Arden of Faversham: A Retelling

David Bruce

Published by David Bruce, 2023.

ARDEN OF FAVERSHAM: A RETELLING

First edition. July 1, 2023.

ISBN: 979-8223825746

Written by David Bruce.

Table of Contents

Dedication

Dedicated to Carl Eugene Bruce and Josephine Saturday Bruce

My father, Carl Eugene Bruce, died on 24 October 2013. He used to work for Ohio Power, and at one time, his job was to shut off the electricity of people who had not paid their bills. He sometimes would find a home with an impoverished mother and some children. Instead of shutting off their electricity, he would tell the mother that she needed to pay her bill or soon her electricity would be shut off. He would write on a form that no one was home when he stopped by because if no one was home he did not have to shut off their electricity.

The best good deed that anyone ever did for my father occurred after a storm that knocked down many power lines. He and other linemen worked long hours and got wet and cold. Their feet were freezing because water got into their boots and soaked their socks. Fortunately, a kind woman gave my father and the other linemen dry socks to wear.

My mother, Josephine Saturday Bruce, died on 14 June 2003. She used to work at a store that sold clothing. One day, an impoverished mother with a baby clothed in rags walked into the store and started shoplifting in an interesting way: The mother took the rags off her baby and dressed the infant in new clothing. My mother knew that this mother could not afford to buy the clothing, but she helped the mother dress her baby and then she watched as the mother walked out of the store without paying.

***

The doing of good deeds is important. As a free person, you can choose to live your life as a good person or as a bad person. To be a good person, do good deeds. To be a bad person, do bad deeds. If you do good deeds, you will become good. If you do bad deeds, you will become bad. To become the person you want to be, act as if you already are that kind of person. Each of us chooses what kind of person we will become. To become a good person, do the things a good person does. To become a bad person, do the things a bad person does. The opportunity to take action to become the kind of person you want to be is yours.

Human beings have free will. According to the Babylonian Niddah 16b, whenever a baby is to be conceived, the Lailah (angel in charge of contraception) takes the drop of semen that will result in the conception and asks God, "Sovereign of the Universe, what is going to be the fate of this drop? Will it develop into a robust or into a weak person? An intelligent or a stupid person? A wealthy or a poor person?" The Lailah asks all these questions, but it does not ask, "Will it develop into a righteous or a wicked person?" The answer to that question lies in the decisions to be freely made by the human being that is the result of the conception.

A Buddhist monk visiting a class wrote this on the chalkboard: "EVERYONE WANTS TO SAVE THE WORLD, BUT NO ONE WANTS TO HELP MOM DO THE DISHES." The students laughed, but the monk then said, "Statistically, it's highly unlikely that any of you will ever have the opportunity to run into a burning orphanage and rescue an infant. But, in the smallest gesture of kindness — a warm smile, holding the door for the person behind you, shoveling the driveway of the elderly person next door — you have committed an act of immeasurable profundity, because to each of us, our life is our universe."

In her book titled *I Have Chosen to Stay and Fight*, comedian Margaret Cho writes, "I believe that we get complimentary snack-size portions of the afterlife, and we all receive them in a different way." For Ms. Cho, many of her snack-size portions of the afterlife come in hip hop music. Other people get different snack-size portions of the afterlife, and we all must be on the lookout for them when they come our way. And perhaps doing good deeds and experiencing good deeds are snack-size portions of the afterlife.

The Zen master Gisan was taking a bath. The water was too hot, so he asked a student to add some cold water to the bath. The student brought a bucket of cold water, added some cold water to the bath, and then threw the rest of the water on a rocky path. Gisan scolded the student: "Everything can be used. Why did you waste the rest of the water by pouring it on the path? There are some plants nearby which could have used the water. What right do you have to waste even a drop of water?" The student became enlightened and changed his name to Tekisui, which means "Drop of Water."

Cover Photograph for *Arden of Faversham*: A Retelling: Pexels https://pixabay.com/photos/woman-knife-model-dangerous-1281651/

***

In this retelling, as in all my retellings, I have tried to make the work of literature accessible to modern readers who may lack some of the knowledge about mythology, religion, and history that the literary work's contemporary audience had.

Do you know a language other than English? If you do, I give you permission to translate this book, copyright your translation, publish or self-publish it, and keep all the royalties for yourself. (Do give me credit, of course, for the original retelling.)

I would like to see my retellings of classic literature used in schools, so I give permission to the country of Finland (and all other countries) to give copies of any or all of my retellings to all students forever. I also give permission to the state of Texas (and all other states) to give copies of any or all of my retellings to all students forever. I also give permission to all teachers to give copies of any or all of my retellings to all students forever. Of course, libraries are welcome to use my eBooks for free.

Teachers need not actually teach my retellings. Teachers are welcome to give students copies of my eBooks as background material. For example, if they are teaching Homer's *Iliad* and *Odyssey*, teachers are welcome to give students copies of my *Virgil's* Aeneid: *A Retelling in Prose* and tell them, "Here's another ancient epic you may want to read in your spare time."

CAST OF CHARACTERS

THOMAS ARDEN, a Gentleman of Faversham.

   ALICE, Wife of Arden.

   MICHAEL, Servant of Arden.

   FRANKLIN, a Friend of Arden.

   MOSBIE, Lover of Alice.

   SUSAN, Mosbie's Sister, and Serving-maid to Alice.

   CLARKE, a Painter.

   ADAM FOWLE, Landlord of the Flower-de-Luce.

   BRADSHAW, a Goldsmith.

   DICK GREENE.

   DICK REEDE.

   A SAILOR, his Friend.

   BLACK WILL, a Murderer.

   GEORGE SHAKEBAG, a Murderer.

   AN APPRENTICE.

   A FERRYMAN.

   LORD CHEINY, and *HIS MEN*

   MAYOR OF FAVERSHAM, and *WATCH*

***

Notes:

   The real-life Arden of Faversham was murdered in 1551.

   In this society, a person of higher rank would use "thou," "thee," "thine," and "thy" when referring to a person of lower rank. (These terms were also used affectionately and between equals.) A person of lower rank would use "you" and "your" when referring to a person of higher rank.

   "Sirrah" was a title used to address someone of a social rank inferior to the speaker. Friends, however, could use it to refer to each other.

   The word "wench" at this time was not necessarily negative. It was often used affectionately.

***

Earliest Extant Edition: 1592

The Tragedy of Master Arden of Faversham. Edited by Martin White. London: Benn; New York: Norton, 1982.

The Tragedy of Master Arden of Faversham. Edited by M. L. Wine. London, Methuen. Distributed in the U. S. A. by Harper & Row Publishers, 1973.

Renaissance Drama : An Anthology of Plays and Entertainments. Edited by Arthur F. Kinney. Malden, MA: Blackwell Pub., 2005.

Arden of Faversham (Arden Early Modern Drama). Edited by Catherine Richardson. London: The Arden Shakespeare, 2022.

Boston University: Willing Suspension Productions Presents Arden of Faversham Written by Anonymous (YouTube)

https://www.youtube.com/watch?v=Oe7-c-EqoOk

CHAPTER 1
— 1.1 —
Scene 1

In a room in Arden's house, Arden and his friend Franklin talked together. Arden was unhappy.

Franklin said:

"Arden, cheer up thy spirits, and droop no more!

"My gracious Lord, the Duke of Somerset, has freely given to thee and to thy heirs, by letters patents from his Majesty, all the lands of the Abbey of Faversham."

He handed Arden the deeds and then said:

"Here are the deeds, sealed and signed with his name and the king's. Read them and leave this melancholy mood."

When the Abbey of Faversham was dissolved, Arden acquired its lands. The Duke of Somerset was the Lord Protector for the young King Edward VI. The letters patents from his Majesty transferred the property into Arden's ownership. It also voided all previous grants and leases of the property.

Arden said:

"Franklin, thy love and friendship prolong my weary life; and except for thee, how odious would be this life, which shows and affords and grants me nothing, but just torments my soul, and how odious would be those foul objects that offend my eyes!

"These things make me wish that, instead of this veil of Heaven — the sky — the earth hung over my head and covered me."

Arden wished that he was dead.

He continued:

"Love-letters have passed between Mosbie and my wife, and they have privy, secret meetings in the town. Indeed, on his finger I saw the ring that on our marriage-day the priest put on her finger.

"Can any grief be half as great as this?"

"Comfort thyself, sweet friend," Franklin said. "It is not strange that women will be false and wavering. Many women cheat on their husbands."

"Aye, but to dote on such a one as he is, is monstrous, Franklin, and it is intolerable," Arden said.

"Why, who is he?" Franklin asked.

Arden said:

"He is a botcher, and he was no better in his origins when he was born."

A botcher mends clothing: It is a low-status job.

Arden continued:

"The man's name is Mosbie, and he was lowly born.

"He, by base brokage getting some small stock, crept into service of a nobleman, and by his servile flattery and fawning, he has now become the steward of his house, and bravely struts and swaggers in his silken gown."

Mosbie got together some small stock — some capital — by working as a broker, which can mean dealing in used clothing; however, the word "brokage" can mean bribing or pimping or engaging in semi-legal business dealings. Mosbie then got work as a nobleman's steward, doing such things as superintending the household servants.

Stewards wore a gown and a chain (necklace), and they carried a white staff.

"No nobleman will countenance and favor such a peasant," Franklin said.

Arden said:

"Yes, the Lord Clifford will; he does not regard me as his friend. But Mosbie better not grow proud through Lord Clifford's favor, for even if Mosbie were backed by the Lord Protector, he should not make me pointed at. I will not allow him to make me an object of ridicule."

By sleeping with Arden's wife, Mosbie could make Arden an object of ridicule.

Arden continued:

"I am well born — I was born a gentleman — and that injurious, insulting, ribald, dissolute rascal, who attempts to violate my dear wife's chastity (for dearly I regard her love, as dear as I regard Heaven) shall on the bed that he thinks to defile see his dissevered and torn-apart joints and sinews, while on the planchers — the floor planks or floorboards — pants his weary body, smeared in the channels and streams of his lustful blood."

Franklin advised:

"Be patient, gentle friend, and learn from me how to ease thy grief and save her chastity:

"Treat and speak to her fairly and gently; sweet words are the fittest engines of war to use to raze and knock to the ground the flint-hard walls of a woman's breast. In any case, don't be too jealous and suspicious and mistrustful, and do not question her love of thee.

"Instead, as if you were completely confident and secure about her, immediately take horse, and ride with me to London to stay with me all this term."

The year was divided into terms: sessions of the law courts.

Franklin continued:

"For women, when they may, will not, but being kept back from doing something, they immediately grow outrageous and furious."

A proverb stated: "Women will be quiet when they are well pleased."

Another proverb stated, "Women will have their wills."

Forbidden fruit is the sweetest. One way to get some teenagers to read a book is to ban it.

Arden said:

"Although this advice is repugnant to reason, yet I'll try it, and call her forth and immediately take leave.

"Alice!"

Arden's wife, Alice, entered the scene and said:

"Husband, why do you get up so early? Summer-nights are short, and yet you rise before dawn.

"If I had been awake, you would not rise so soon."

The verb "rise" may have the additional meaning of "get a penile erection."

Alice's words are ambiguous: 1) If I had been awake, you would not have gotten an erection, and 2) If I had been awake, you would not rise out of bed so soon because I would put your erection to use.

Arden said:

"Sweet love, thou know that we two, Ovid-like, have often chidden the morning when it began to peep, and we have often wished that dark Night's purblind steeds would pull back Dawn by the purple mantle and cast her in the ocean to her love."

Lovers tend to wish the night to be prolonged and for dawn to be delayed. The lover in Ovid's *Amores* I.13 does this. Juliet in Shakespeare's *Romeo and Juliet* does this on her wedding night. In Homer's *Odyssey*, the goddess Athena holds back the dawn so that Odysseus and Penelope have time to talk together and have sex and sleep.

Night is personified as a driver of horses pulling a chariot. Purblind horses are thoroughly or partially blind horses. Dawn's purple mantle is the color of the dawn as the sun rises.

The Greek goddess of the dawn was Eos, one of whose lovers was Tithonus.

Arden continued:

"But this night, sweet Alice, thou have killed my heart: I heard thee call on Mosbie in thy sleep.

"It is likely I was asleep when I named him, for when I am awake, he does not come into my thoughts," Alice said.

"Aye, but you started up and suddenly, instead of him, you caught me about the neck," Arden said.

"Instead of him?" Alice said. "Why, who was there but you? And where there is only one man, how can I be mistaken about which man he is?"

"Arden, cease to urge her over-far," Franklin said. "Don't push her too hard."

Arden said:

"Indeed, love, there is no credit and truth in a dream."

A proverb stated: Dreams are lies.

Arden continued:

"Let it suffice that I know thou love me well."

"Now I remember from where it came," Alice said. "Didn't we talk about Mosbie last night?"

"Mistress Alice, I heard you name him once or twice," Franklin said.

"And from there the dream came, and therefore don't blame me," Alice said.

Arden said:

"I know it did, and therefore I let it pass. I pay it no attention.

"I must go to London, sweet Alice, immediately."

"But tell me, do you mean to stay there long?" Alice asked.

"I will be there no longer than my affairs are done," Arden said.

"He will not stay above a month at most," Franklin said.

"A month? Woe to me!" Alice said. "Sweet Arden, return home again within a day or two, or else I die."

Arden said:

"I cannot long be away from thee, gentle Alice.

"While our servant Michael fetches our horses from the field, Franklin and I will go down to the quay — the wharf — for I have certain goods there to unload.

"Meanwhile prepare our breakfast, gentle Alice; for yet before noon we'll take to our horses and ride away."

Arden and Franklin exited.

Alice said to herself:

"Before noon he means to take to his horse and ride away! Sweet news is this. Oh, that some airy, immaterial spirit would in the shape and likeness of a horse gallop with Arden across the ocean and throw him from his back into the waves!

"Sweet Mosbie is the man who has my heart.

"And my husband, Arden, usurps it, having no claim on me but this: I am tied to him by marriage.

"Love is a god, and marriage is only words, and therefore Mosbie's title is the best."

The god called Love is Cupid.

Alice continued saying to herself:

"Bah! Whether or not Mosbie's title is the best, he shall be mine, in spite of Arden, of Hymen, and of marriage rites."

Hymen is the god of marriage.

Adam Fowle entered the scene. Adam was the landlord of the inn called Flower-de-Luce, where Mosbie stayed when he was at Faversham.

Alice continued saying to herself:

"And here comes Adam of the Flower-de-Luce. I hope he brings me tidings of my love."

She said out loud:

"How are things now, Adam? What is the news with you?

"Don't be afraid to speak; my husband is now away from home."

Adam brought messages to her from Mosbie.

"He whom you know — Mosbie — Mistress Alice, has come to town, and he sends you word by me that no matter what you may not visit him," Adam said.

"Not visit him?" Alice asked.

"No, nor take any knowledge of his being here," Adam said.

"But tell me, is he angry or displeased?" Alice asked.

"It would seem so, for he is wondrously sad," Adam said.

Alice said:

"Even if he were as mad as raving Hercules, I'll see him, I will."

In a fit of madness caused by the goddess Hera, who hated him, Hercules killed his wife and children. Hercules' story is told in Euripides' tragedy *Heracles*. Hercules' Greek name is Heracles.

Alice continued:

"And even if thy house — thy inn — were fortified, these hands of mine would raze it to the ground, unless thou would bring me to my love."

"Nay, if you are so impatient, I'll be gone," Adam said.

Alice said:

"Stay, Adam, stay; thou were accustomed to be my friend.

"Ask Mosbie how I have incurred his wrath. Bear to him from me this pair of silver dice, with which we played for kisses many a time. And when I lost, I won, and so did he. May Jove send me such winning and such losing!

"And bid him, if his love does not decline, to come this morning just along — past — my door, and as if he were a stranger, just greet me there.

"This he may do without suspicion or fear."

"I'll tell him what you say, and so farewell," Adam said.

"Do, and one day I'll make amends for all," Alice said.

Adam exited.

Alone, Alice said to herself:

"I know he loves me well, but he dares not come because my husband is so jealous, and these my narrow-prying neighbors blab, and so they hinder our meetings when we would converse.

"But, if I live, that block shall be removed."

A "block" is 1) an obstruction, and/or 2) a hard-hearted person, and/or 3) a blockhead.

Alone, Alice continued saying to herself:

"And, Mosbie, thou who come to me by stealth, shall neither fear the biting speech of men, nor Arden's looks; as surely he shall die as I abhor him and love only thee."

Michael, Arden's servant, entered the scene.

"How are things now, Michael?" Alice asked. "Where are you going?

"To fetch my master's nag," Michael said. "I hope you'll think about and remember me."

"Aye; but, Michael, see that you keep your oath, and be as secret as you are resolute," Alice said.

"I'll see that he shall not live above a week," Michael said.

"On that condition, Michael, here is my hand," Alice said. "None shall have Mosbie's sister but thyself."

"I understand the painter here nearby has made report that he and Sue are sure — that they are betrothed," Michael said.

"There's no such thing, Michael," Alice said. "Don't believe it."

Michael said:

"But he has sent her an emblem of a dagger sticking in a heart, with a verse or two stolen — that is, plagiarized — from a painted cloth. I hear the wench keeps the emblem in her chest."

Woven tapestries are more valuable than painted tapestries.

Michael continued:

"Well, let her keep it! I shall find a fellow who can both write and read and make rhymes, too.

"And if I do — well, I say no more. I'll send from London such a taunting letter that she shall eat the heart he sent with salt and fling the dagger at the painter's head."

"Why do all this?" Alice said. "I say that Susan's thine."

"Why, then I say that I will kill my master, or anything that you will have me do," Michael said.

"But, Michael, see that you do it cunningly," Alice said.

"Why, say I should be taken and arrested, I'll never confess that you know anything," Michael said, "and Susan, being a maiden, may beg me from the gallows of the shrieve: the sheriff."

Michael believed that he could be saved from hanging if a virgin — Susan — offered to marry him.

"Don't trust to that, Michael," Alice said.

Michael said:

"You can't tell me what not to do: I have seen it, I have.

"But, mistress, tell her, whether I live or die, I'll make her wealthier than twenty painters can. For I will get rid of my elder brother by killing him, and then the farm of Bolton is my own.

"Who would not venture upon house and land, when he may have it for a downright blow?"

Mosbie entered the scene.

Alice said:

"Yonder comes Mosbie. Michael, get thee gone, and don't let him nor anyone else know thy drifts and schemes."

Michael exited.

Alice then said:

"Mosbie, my love!"

"Go away, I say, and don't talk to me now," Mosbie said.

"A word or two, sweetheart, and then I will," Alice said. "It is yet but early in the day; thou need not fear."

"Where is your husband?" Mosbie asked.

"It is now high water — high tide — and he is at the key," Alice said.

The key is a quad, aka wharf.

"There let him be," Mosbie said. "Henceforward do not know me."

Alice said:

"Is this the end of all thy solemn oaths? Is this quarrel the fruit thy reconcilement causes to bud?

"Have I for this given thee so many favors, incurred my husband's hate, and — alas! — have I made shipwreck of my honor for thy sake? And do thou say, 'Henceforward do not know me?'

"Remember, when I locked thee in my closet — my private room — what were thy words and mine. Didn't we both decree to murder Arden in the night? The heavens can witness, and the world can tell, before I saw that falsehood look of thine, before I was entangled with thy enticing speech, Arden to me was dearer than my soul — and he shall be still and always.

"Base peasant, get thee gone, and don't boast of thy conquest over me, gotten by witchcraft and sheer sorcery!

"For what have thou to countenance — to be in keeping with — my love, I being descended of a noble family, and married already to a gentleman whose servant thou could be!

"And so I say farewell to you."

Mosbie said:

"Ungentle and unkind Alice, now I see that which I always feared and find too true: A woman's love is as the lightning-flame, which even in bursting forth consumes itself.

"To test thy constancy I have been strange and distant to thee. I wish that I had never tested your love but had instead lived in hope!"

"Why do thou need to test me, whom thou never found false?" Alice asked.

"Yet pardon me, for love is jealous," Mosbie said.

Alice said:

"So listens the sailor to the mermaid's song. So looks the traveler to the basilisk."

In this society, mermaids were conflated with Sirens, who sang beautifully to lure sailors to their death.

Looking into the eyes of a basilisk, the king of serpents, was fatal.

Alice continued:

"I am content to be reconciled to thee, and that, I know, will be my overthrow and ruin."

"Thine overthrow and ruin?" Mosbie said. "First let the world dissolve."

"Nay, Mosbie, let me still and always enjoy thy love, and I am resolute whatever happens," Alice said. "My saving husband hoards up bags of gold to make our children rich, and now he has gone to unload the goods that shall be thine, and he and Franklin will go to London immediately."

"To London, Alice?" Mosbie said. "If thou shall be ruled by me and take my advice, we'll make him sure enough before coming there."

In other words: We'll kill him and prevent him from going there.

"Ah, I wish that we could!" Alice said.

Mosbie said:

"I happened on a painter yesterday, the only cunning — the cleverest in magic — man of Christendom. For he can mix poison with his oil, so that whosoever looks upon the work he paints shall, with the beams that issue from his sight, suck venom to his breast and slay himself."

This society believed that eyes emit beams that enabled them to see.

Mosbie continued:

"Sweet Alice, he shall draw thy counterfeit — thy portrait — so that Arden may, by gazing on it, perish."

"Aye, but Mosbie, that is dangerous," Alice said, "for thou, or I, or anyone else, coming into the chamber where it hangs, may die."

"Aye, but we'll have it covered with a cloth and hung up in the study for he himself to look at," Mosbie said.

"It may not be, for once the picture's drawn and completed, Arden, I know, will come and show it to me," Alice said.

Mosbie said:

"Fear not; we'll have something that shall serve the turn — we'll find a way to get around that obstacle."

Mosbie and Alice had been walking in the street, and Mosbie said:

"This is the painter's house; I'll call him forth."

Alice said, "But Mosbie, I'll have no such picture — I won't."

Mosbie said:

"Please, leave it to my discretion. I'll take care of it."

He then called to the painter:

"Hey! Clarke!"

Clarke, an artist of Faversham, came out of his house.

Mosbie said to him:

"Oh, you are an honest man of your word! You served me well."

Clarke said:

"Why, sir, I'll do it for you at any time, provided, as you have given your word, I may have Susan Mosbie to be my wife."

This is the same Susan whom Michael wanted to marry.

Clarke continued:

"For, as sharp-witted poets, whose sweet verse makes heavenly gods break off their nectar draughts and lay their ears down to the lowly earth, use humble promise to — that is, are inspired by — their sacred Muse, so we who are the poets' favorites and intimates must have a love. Aye, Love is the painter's Muse that makes him frame and fashion a speaking countenance and face, a weeping eye that witnesses heart's grief."

Poets have Muses to inspire them to create work that will make even the gods pay admiring attention. Artists have the god of Love — Cupid — to inspire them to create expressive and moving art.

Clarke said:

"Then tell me, Master Mosbie, shall I have her?"

"It would be a pity if he did not get her," Alice said. "He'll treat her well."

"Clarke, here's my hand. My sister shall be thine," Mosbie said.

"Then, brother, to requite this courtesy and repay you, you shall command my life, my skill, and all," Clarke said.

Clark expected to be Mosbie's brother-in-law soon.

"Ah, that thou could be secret," Alice said.

She worried that he would not keep their plot to kill her husband secret.

Mosbie said to Alice, "Don't fear him. Stop talking about it; I have talked sufficiently."

Clarke said to Alice:

"You who ask such questions don't know me.

"Let it suffice that I know you love Mosbie well, and you eagerly would have your husband made away and killed. Wherein, trust me. You show a noble mind: Rather than you'll live with him you hate, you'll venture and risk your life, and die with him you love.

"The like I will do for my Susan's sake."

Alice said:

"Yet nothing could force me to do this deed except Mosbie's love."

She then said to Mosbie:

"If I might without control and restraint enjoy thee always, then Arden should not die. But seeing I cannot, therefore let him die."

Mosbie said to her:

"Enough, sweet Alice; thy kind words make me melt; tears are coming into my eyes."

He then said to Clarke:

"Your trick of poisoned pictures we dislike. Some other poison would do far better."

"Aye, such as might be put into his broth and yet is not to be found in taste at all," Alice said.

"I know your mind, and here I have it for you," Clarke said. "Put just a dram — a tiny bit — of this into his drink, or any kind of broth that he shall eat, and he shall die within an hour after."

Clarke gave Alice a small vial of poison.

"As I am a gentlewoman, Clarke, the next day thou and Susan shall be married," Alice said.

"And I'll make her dowry more than I'll talk of right now, Clarke," Mosbie said.

Mosbie was Susan's brother.

Clarke said to Alice:

"Yonder's your husband."

He then said:

"Mosbie, I'll be gone."

Clarke exited.

Alice said quietly:

"He leaves at a good time. See where my husband comes."

Having returned from the wharf, Arden and Franklin walked over to them.

Alice said out loud:

"Master Mosbie, ask him the question yourself."

She was pretending that Mosbie had asked her something that her husband could answer. Mosbie was quick-witted enough to invent such a question.

Mosbie said:

"Master Arden, being at London last night, the Abbey lands, whereof you are now possessed and own, were offered to me during a chance meeting by Dick Greene, one of Sir Antony Ager's men.

"Please, sir, tell me, aren't the lands yours? Have you any other interest herein? Is the ownership of the lands disputed?"

Arden said:

"Mosbie, that question we'll settle soon."

He then turned to his wife and said:

"Alice, make my breakfast. I must go away from here."

Alice exited.

Arden then said:

"As for the lands, Mosbie, they are mine by letters patents from his Majesty.

"But I must have a mandate for — a deed of possession of — my wife. They say you seek to rob me of her love."

Arden now began to refer to Mosbie using *thou*, *thee*, and *thy* rather than the respectful *you*:

"Villain, what are thou doing in her company? She's no companion for so base a groom: so base a low servant."

Mosbie said, "Arden, I was not thinking about seeing her. I came to see thee. But rather than I pocket up and ignore this wrong —"

Franklin interrupted, "— what will you do, sir?"

"Revenge it on the proudest of you both," Mosbie said.

Moving quickly, Arden drew Mosbie's sword from out of its scabbard and said:

"So, sirrah; you may not wear a sword. The statute decrees against artificers."

"Artificers" are 1) craftsmen, and/or 2) tricksters.

A statute made it illegal for a man below the rank of gentleman to wear a sword.

Arden continued:

"I warrant that I do."

Arden, who was a gentleman, did legally wear a sword. He also believed that he was legally entitled to take away Mosbie's sword.

Mosbie's social rank was goodman, which was just below the rank of gentleman.

Arden continued:

"Now use your bodkin, your Spanish needle, and your pressing iron, for this sword of yours shall go with me; and mark my words, you goodman botcher, it is to you I speak."

Mosbie had been a botcher — a mender of clothes — and a bodkin (used for making holes in cloth), a Spanish needle, and a pressing iron were tools of the trade.

Arden continued:

"The next time that I catch thee near my house, instead of thee walking on legs I'll make thee crawl on stumps."

"Ah, Master Arden, you have injured me," Mosbie said. "I do appeal to God and to the world."

"Why, can thou deny thou were a botcher once?" Franklin asked.

"Measure me — judge me — by what I am, not by what I was," Mosbie said.

"Why, what are thou now but a velvet drudge, a cheating steward, and a base-minded peasant?" Arden asked.

A velvet drudge is a well-dressed servant.

Mosbie said:

"Arden, now that thou have belched and vomited the rancorous, animosity-filled venom of thy mis-swollen heart, just hear me speak."

Arden's heart was swollen with anger, and Mosbie was lying when he said that Arden had no good reason to be angry.

Mosbie continued:

"As I intend to live with God and his elected — chosen by God Himself — saints in Heaven, I never meant anymore to solicit and pursue her; and that she knows, and all the world shall see.

"I loved her once. Sweet Arden, pardon me. I couldn't choose not to love her — her beauty fired my heart! But time has quenched these over-raging coals; and, Arden, although I now frequent thy house, it is for my sister's sake, her waiting-maid, and not for the sake of Alice.

"May thou enjoy her long. May Hell-fire and wrathful vengeance alight on me, if I dishonor her or injure thee."

Arden said:

"Mosbie, the deadly hatred of my heart is appeased with these thy protestations and avowals, and thou and I'll be friends, if this proves to be true.

"As for the base, insulting terms that I gave thee just now, forget them, Mosbie. I had reason to speak them when all the knights and gentlemen of Kent make common table-talk and gossip about her and thee."

"Who lives who is not touched with slanderous tongues?" Mosbie asked.

"Then, Mosbie, to stop the speech and gossip of men, upon whose general bruit and rumor all honor hangs, stay away from his house," Franklin said.

"Stay away from it!" Arden said. "Nay, rather frequent it more. The world shall see that I don't distrust my wife. To warn him on the sudden to stay away from my house would be to confirm the rumor that has grown."

Mosbie said, "By my faith, sir, you say the truth, and therefore I will sojourn and stay here a while, until our enemies have talked their fill, and then, I hope, they'll cease, and at last confess how causeless and without reason they have injured her and me."

Arden said:

"And I will stay at London all this term to let them see how lightly I weigh their words."

Alice returned with Arden's breakfast.

She said, "Husband, sit down; your breakfast will be cold."

"Come, Master Mosbie, will you sit with us?" Arden asked.

"I cannot eat, but I'll sit for company," Mosbie said.

"Sirrah Michael, see that our horses are ready," Arden ordered.

Michael exited.

Arden tasted the broth, but then he stopped eating.

"Husband, why do you pause?" Alice asked. "Why don't you eat?"

"I am not well," Arden said. "There's something in this broth that is not wholesome. Did thou make it, Alice?"

Alice said:

"I did, and that's the reason it doesn't please you."

She threw the broth on the floor, and then she said:

"There's nothing I do that can please your taste. It would be best for you to say that I would have poisoned you.

"I cannot speak or look around, but he imagines I have stepped awry and committed adultery. Here's the man — Mosbie — whom you cast in my teeth and face so often.

"Now I will either be convicted or be purged of suspicion."

She then said to Mosbie:

"I order thee to speak to this mistrustful man, thou who would see me hang, thou, Mosbie, thou.

"What favor have thou had more than a kiss at coming or departing from the town?"

In this society, it was customary for people of the opposite sex to kiss when meeting or departing.

"You wrong yourself and me to cast these doubts and suspicions," Mosbie said. "Your loving husband is not jealous."

Arden said:

"Why, gentle Mistress Alice, can't I be ill, but you'll accuse yourself?"

He then said:

"Franklin, thou have a box of mithridate; I'll take a little to prevent the worst."

Mithridate is a universal antidote to poison.

"Do so and let us immediately get on horseback and depart for London," Franklin said. "I bet my life against yours that you shall do well enough."

Alice said:

"Give me a spoon — I'll eat of it myself. I wish that it were full of poison to the brim. Then my cares and troubles would have an end."

Alice had already thrown the broth on the floor, so she could not eat it.

Alice continued:

"Was ever a silly — a simple, powerless — woman so tormented?"

"Be patient, sweet love," Arden said. "I don't mistrust thee."

"God will revenge it, Arden, if thou do," Alice said, "for a woman never loved her husband better than I love thee."

"I know it, sweet Alice," Arden said. "Cease to complain, lest in tears I answer thee again."

"Come, leave this dallying, and let us go away," Franklin said.

"Forbear to wound me with that bitter word — 'away,'" Alice said. "Arden shall go to London in my arms."

"I am loath to depart, yet I must go," Arden said.

Alice said:

"Will thou go to London, then, and leave me here? Ah, if thou love me, gentle Arden, stay.

"Yet, if thy business be of great import, go, if thou will; I'll bear it as I may. But write from London to me every week, nay, every day, and stay no longer there than thou need to, lest I die for sorrow."

"I'll write to thee every other tide," Arden said, "and so farewell, sweet Alice, until we next meet."

The tide ebbs and flows twice a lunar day, so Arden will write her once a day.

Alice replied:

"Farewell, husband, seeing you'll have it so."

She then said:

"And, Master Franklin, seeing you take him hence, in hope you'll hasten him to come home, I'll give you this."

She kissed him.

She then said:

"Mosbie, farewell, and see that you keep your oath."

"I hope he is not jealous of me now," Mosbie said.

"And if he stays in London longer than he needs to, the fault shall not be mine," Franklin said.

"No, Mosbie, no," Arden said. "Hereafter think of me as of your dearest friend, and so farewell."

Arden and Franklin exited.

Alice said to Mosbie, "I am glad he is gone; he was about to stay, but did you see then how I broke off?"

Alice had been convincing in her acting. If she had continued to ask her husband to stay, her husband may have stayed.

Mosbie said, "Aye, Alice, and it was cunningly performed. But what a villain is this painter Clarke!"

Clark had concocted a faulty poison: one whose taste could be detected with one spoonful of poisoned food.

Alice said:

"Wasn't it a 'good' poison that he gave me?

"Why, my husband is as healthy now as he was before.

"The painter should have given me some fine confection — some fine poisonous mixture — that might have given the broth some dainty, pleasant taste. This powder was too gross and palpable: too obvious and perceptible."

"But had he eaten just three spoonfuls more, then he would have died, and our love would have continued," Mosbie said.

"Why, so it shall, Mosbie, even though my husband is still alive," Alice said.

"It is impossible, for I have sworn never hereafter to solicit and court thee, or, while he lives, once more to importune and chase thee," Mosbie said.

Alice said:

"Thou shall not need to because I will importune and chase thee. What! Shall an oath make thee forsake my love? As if I have not sworn as much myself and given my hand to him in the church!

"Bah, Mosbie; oaths are words, and words are wind, and wind is mutable — changeable. So then, I conclude, it is childishness to stand upon an oath."

This is Alice's argument.

P1: A promise is made up of words.

P2: Words are like the wind.

P3: The wind is never constant: It is changeable.

C: A promise is changeable.

P4: If a promise is changeable, then it is childish to keep it.

C2: It is childish to stand upon an oath and insist that a promise must be kept.

She was making an argument from analogy: Words are like the wind. But critics can say that it is a weak argument from analogy: The analogy between words and promises is not strong.

"Well proved, Mistress Alice," Mosbie said, "yet by your leave and with your permission, I'll keep my oath unbroken while he lives."

This society took oaths and damnation seriously. Mosbie's oath to Arden was this: "May Hell-fire and wrathful vengeance alight on me, if I dishonor her or injure thee."

Mosbie truly believed that if he broke his oath, eternal damnation would follow.

Alice said:

"Aye, do, and spare not. His time is but short."

In other words: Go ahead and keep your oath; Arden has not much longer to live.

Alice continued:

"For if thou should be as resolute as I, we'll have him murdered as he walks the streets.

"In London ruffians frequent many alehouses. These ruffians, I hear, will murder men for gold. They shall be soundly given fees to pay him home."

In other words: The ruffians shall be well-paid to kill Arden.

Dick Greene entered the scene.

"Alice, who's he who comes yonder?" Mosbie asked. "Do thou know him?"

"Mosbie, leave," Alice said. "I hope it is one who comes to put in practice our intended drifts — to execute our plots."

Mosbie exited.

Dick Greene said:

"Mistress Arden, you are well met. I am pleased to see you.

"I am sorry that your husband is away from home because my purposed journey was to see him. Yet all my labor is not spent in vain, for I suppose that you can fully explain and completely satisfy me about the thing I seek."

"What is it, Master Greene?" Alice said. "If I may or can help you with safety, I will answer you."

Dick Greene said:

"I heard your husband has the grant recently, confirmed by letters patents from the king, of all the lands of the Abbey of Faversham. I heard that Arden is generally entitled — furnished with a title — and is in complete possession of these lands, so that all former grants are cut off and superseded; of which I myself had one.

"But if what I heard is true, now my interest by that is void.

"This is all, Mistress Arden. Is what I have heard true or not?"

Alice said:

"It is true, Master Greene; the lands are his in state — that is, by law; he has legal possession and ownership of them. And whatsoever leases were in existence before are void for the duration of Master Arden's life."

Alice was lying in part. The lands belonged to Arden's heirs after his death. Alice wanted to persuade Greene to kill Arden. If he thought that he could get his grant back, he might do that.

Alice continued:

"My husband has the grant under the seal of the Court of the Lord Chancellor."

Next to the House of Lords, this was the highest court in the land.

Dick Greene said:

"Pardon me, Mistress Arden, I must speak for I am touched and affected by this. Your husband does me wrong to wring from me the little land I have. My living — that is, my lands — is my life, and only my lands are the remainder of my portion."

"Mistress Arden" means "Mrs. Arden."

The lands that were now owned by Arden were the lands that had been all that remained of Greene's inheritance. Those lands had been his living: He had received all his income from them.

Dick Greene continued:

"Desire of wealth is endless in his mind, and he is greedy-gaping always for gain. Nor does he care if young gentlemen are forced to beg, as long as he may scrape and hoard up wealth in his moneybag. But, seeing he has taken my lands, I'll value life as carelessly as he is careful to get wealth."

Arden much values wealth; because Greene now lacks adequate income to be a gentleman, Greene little values life and is willing to risk his life to get revenge against Arden.

Dick Greene continued:

"And tell him this from me, I'll be revenged to such an extent that he shall wish the Abbey lands had rested still within their former state and with their former owners."

"Alas, poor gentleman, I pity you," Alice said, "and I am sorry that any man should want and lack! God knows it is not my fault; but don't wonder that he is hard to others, when to me — ah, Master Greene, God knows how I am treated."

Dick Greene said:

"Why, Mistress Arden, can the crabbed, perverse churl treat you unkindly? Doesn't he respect your birth, your honorable friends, nor what you brought to him?

"Why, all Kent knows your parentage and who you are. He should treat you well because of your family, your friends, and the dowry you brought to him."

Alice said:

"Ah, Master Greene, let it be spoken in secret here. I never live a good day with him alone.

"When he is at home, then I receive froward, hateful looks, hard words, and blows to 'mend' the marriage match with, and although I might as a wife make content as good a man as he is, yet he keeps in every corner trulls."

"Trulls" and "trugs" are prostitutes.

Alice continued:

"And when he's weary with his trugs at home here in Faversham, then he rides straight to London; there, indeed, he revels it among such filthy people who advise him to make away — to kill — his wife.

"Thus I live daily in continual fear, in sorrow, and so despairing of redress and remedy that every day I wish with hearty prayer that he or I were taken from the world."

Dick Greene said:

"Now trust me, Mistress Alice, it grieves me that so beautiful a creature as you should be so abused.

"Why, who would have thought the seemingly civil sir to be so sullen and capable of ill humor? He looks so smooth — so courteous and affable.

"Now, shame on him, that churl! And if he lives a day longer, he lives too long.

"But be frolicsome, woman! I shall be the man who shall set you free from all this discontent and unhappiness; and if the churl denies my interest — my legal right to the property — and will not yield my lease into my hand, I'll pay him home and get my revenge, whatever happens to me."

Greene had no legal right to the property; Arden did have the legal right to the property.

"But do you speak as you think?" Alice asked. "Do you mean what you say?"

"Aye, as God's my witness, I mean plain dealing, for I had rather die than lose my land," Dick Greene said. "I do mean what I say."

Alice said:

"Then, Master Greene, be counseled by me: Take my advice.

"Don't endanger yourself for such a churl but hire some cutter — some cutthroat — to cut his life short, and here's ten pounds to pay the cutters with. When my husband is dead, you shall have twenty more pounds, and the lands whereof my husband is possessed shall be entitled as they were before."

"Will you keep your promise to me? " Dick Greene asked.

"If I don't, then account me false and perjured while I live," Alice said.

"Then here's my hand, I'll have him so dispatched," Dick Greene said. "I'll go up to London immediately, I'll go thither posthaste, and never rest until I have accomplished it. Until then, farewell."

Alice said:

"May good fortune follow all your forward, eager thoughts."

Dick Greene exited.

Now four people were willing to kill Arden: Alice, Mosbie, Michael, and Dick Greene.

Alice said to herself:

"And whosoever does attempt the deed, a happy hand I wish, and so farewell.

"All this goes well.

"Mosbie, I long for thee so I can let thee know all that I have contrived."

Mosbie and Clarke entered the scene.

"How are things now, Alice?" Mosbie asked. "What's the news?"

"Such as will content thee well, sweetheart," Alice said.

Mosbie said, "Well, let the news remain unspoken for a while, and tell me now, Alice, have you dealt with and persuaded my sister to marry Clarke? Will she have my neighbor Clarke, or not?"

Alice said:

"What, Master Mosbie! Let him woo her himself! Do you think that maidens don't look for fair words?"

She then said:

"Go to her, Clarke; she's all alone inside.

"Michael, my serving-man, is clean out of her books. Michael is completely out of favor with her."

"I thank you, Mistress Arden, I will go in," Clarke said, "and if fair Susan and I can make a marriage agreement, you shall command me to the uttermost, as far as either goods or life may stretch.

Clarke exited.

"Now, Alice, let's hear thy news," Mosbie said.

"My news is so good that I must laugh for joy before I can begin to tell my tale," Alice said.

"Let's hear the news so that I may laugh and keep you company," Mosbie said.

Alice said:

"This morning, Master Greene — Dick Greene, I mean — from whom my husband had the Abbey land, came hither, railing and complaining, in order to know the truth of whether my husband had the lands by grant.

"I told him all, whereat he stormed amain — violently — and swore he would cry quittance — that is, get even — with the churl, and, if my husband did deny his interest, stab him, no matter what befell to himself.

"When I saw his choler and anger rise thus, I whetted and further incited the gentleman with words, and, to conclude, Mosbie, at last we grew to composition for my husband's death."

The composition was a contract: Greene would kill Arden, and Alice would reward him with wealth.

Alice continued:

"I gave him ten pounds to use to hire knaves to, by some scheme, kill the churl, and when Arden is dead, Greene should have twenty more pounds and repossess his former lands again.

"On this we agreed, and he has ridden straightaway to London, in order to bring Arden's death about."

"But do you call this good news?" Mosbie asked.

"Aye, sweetheart," Alice said. "Isn't this good news?"

Mosbie said:

"It would be cheerful news to hear that the churl was dead.

"But trust me, Alice. I take it surpassingly ill that you would be so forgetful of our situation that you recount it to every man.

"What! To acquaint each stranger with our plans, chiefly in the case of murder, why, it is the way to make it open and known to Arden himself and bring both thyself and me to ruin.

"Forewarned is forearmed; the man who threatens his enemy lends him a sword to use to guard himself."

"I did it for the best," Alice said.

"Well, seeing it is done, let us cheerfully let it pass," Mosbie said. "You know this Greene; isn't he religious? A man, I guess, of great devotion?"

"He is," Alice said.

"Then, sweet Alice, let it pass," Mosbie said. "I have a scheme that will quiet all, whatever is amiss."

Clarke returned, accompanied by Susan.

"How are things now, Clarke?" Alice asked. "Have you found me false? Did I lie to you? Didn't I plead the matter hard for you?"

"You did," Clarke said.

"And what is the result?" Mosbie asked. "Will it be a marriage match?"

Clarke said:

"A marriage match, indeed, sir. Aye, the day is mine. I have won the day.

"The painter lays his colors to the life. His pencil draws no shadows in his love."

In other words: I am the painter, and I have painted a metaphorical picture with lots of bright colors and no shadow: All is well.

A "pencil" is a small paintbrush with a pointed tip.

Clarke concluded:

"Susan is mine."

"You make her blush," Alice said.

"What do you say, sister?" Mosbie asked. "Is it Clarke who must be the man you marry?"

"It rests in your grant," Susan said. "Some words passed between us, and happily we have grown into a match, if you are willing that it shall be so."

In other words: They had agreed to be married, and all that was needed was Mosbie's consent.

Mosbie said, "Ah, Master Clarke, it rests at my grant: You see my sister's yet at my disposal, but, as long as you'll grant me one thing I shall ask, I am content that my sister shall be yours."

"What is it, Master Mosbie?" Clarke asked.

Mosbie said:

"I remember once in secret talk, you told me how you could compound by art — skillfully create — a poisoned crucifix that whosoever looked upon it should grow blind and with the scent be stifled — suffocated. And that before long whoever viewed it well should die poisoned.

"I would have you make me such a crucifix, and then I'll grant my sister shall be yours."

Clarke said, "Although I am loath, because it touches life — it involves murder — yet rather than I'll leave sweet Susan's love, I'll do it, and with all the haste I may. But for whom is it?"

Alice said:

"Leave that to us.

"Why, Clarke, is it possible that you should paint and draw it out yourself, with the colors being baleful and malignant and poisoned, and yet you in no ways injure yourself while creating it?"

Mosbie said:

"Well questioned, Alice.

"Clarke, how do you answer that question?"

Clarke said:

"Very easily. I'll tell you straightaway how I work with these poisoned drugs.

"I fasten on my spectacles so close that nothing can in any way offend and hurt my sight. Then, just as I put a leaf within my nose, so I put rhubarb to avoid the smell."

One kind of leaf that is put in the nose is tobacco leaf (in the form of smoke).

Rhubarb leaves and flowers are scented.

Clarke may have smoked rhubarb leaves or burned them in his studio.

This society believed that tobacco and rhubarb had medicinal qualities.

Clarke concluded:

"The result is that I paint it as softly — as easily — as I would paint another, non-poisoned work."

"It is very well," Mosbie said, "but when shall I have it?"

"Within the next ten days," Clarke said.

Mosbie said:

"It will serve the turn and meet the situation."

Clarke exited.

Mosbie then said:

"Now, Alice, let's go in and see what cheer — what food and drink — you keep.

"I hope, now Master Arden is away from home, you'll give me permission to play your husband's part."

That included the husband's part in bed.

"Mosbie, you know that who is the master of my heart well may become the master of the house," Alice said.

CHAPTER 2
— 2.1 —
Scene 2

In the country between Faversham and London, Dick Greene and a goldsmith named Bradshaw talked together.

"Do you see them who come yonder, Master Greene?" Bradshaw asked.

"Aye, very well," Dick Greene said. "Do you know them?"

Black Will and Shakebag entered the scene and walked toward them.

Bradshaw said:

"The one I don't know, but he seems a knave chiefly for bearing the other company. For the other man is such a slave that so vile a rogue as he lives not again upon the earth. Black Will is his name, I tell you, Master Greene. At Boulogne, he and I were fellow-soldiers."

Bradshaw and Black Will had served together in the 1544 campaign of King Henry VIII, when the king besieged and captured Boulogne, a French port town on the English Channel.

Bradshaw continued:

"There he played such pranks — such bad deeds — that all the camp feared him for his villainy. I promise you that he bears so bad a mind that for a crown he'll murder any man."

A crown is a coin worth five shillings. It was called a crown because it had the image of a crown stamped on one side.

Dick Greene said to himself, "The fitter is he for my purpose, by the Virgin Mary!"

"How are you now, fellow Bradshaw?" Black Will asked. "Where are you going so early?"

"O Will, times have changed," Bradshaw said. "We are no longer fellows now, although we were once together in the field. Yet I am thy friend and will do thee any good I can."

Bradshaw was a goldsmith now, while Black Will was a criminal.

Black Will said:

"Why, Bradshaw, weren't thou and I fellow-soldiers at Boulogne, where I was a corporal, and thou were only a base mercenary groom: a lowly soldier? We are not fellows now because you are a goldsmith and have a little gold and silver plate in your shop!

"You were then glad to call me 'fellow Will,' and with a curtesy — a bow — to the earth, you said, 'One snatch — one bit of food — good corporal,' when I stole the half-ox from John the vitler, and you domineered — feasted and reveled — with it among good fellows and companions in one night."

A "vitler" is a provider of food. "Vittles" are food.

"Aye, Will, those days are past with me," Bradshaw said.

Black Will said:

"Aye, but they are not past with me, for I keep that same honorable mind still.

"Good neighbor Bradshaw, you are too proud to be my fellow; but were it not that I see more company — more people — coming down the hill, I would be fellows with you once more, and share crowns with you, too. But let that pass and tell me whither you go."

"To London, Will, about a piece of service, wherein perhaps thou may pleasure me," Bradshaw said.

In other words: Bradshaw was seeking help, and Black Will might be able to help him.

"What is it?" Black Will asked.

Bradshaw said:

"Recently, Lord Cheiny lost some plate, which someone brought to and sold at my shop, saying he was the servant of Sir Antony Cooke. A search was made, the plate was found with me, and I am bound to answer at the assize."

Bradshaw had been accused of receiving stolen property, and he had to appear before authorities to explain how he had come into possession of the gold and silver plate. He was hoping that Black Will could tell him who had stolen the gold and silver plate.

Bradshaw continued:

"Now, Lord Cheiny solemnly vows that if law will serve him, he'll hang me for the theft of his plate.

"Now, I am going to London, hoping to find the fellow.

"Now, Will, I know thou are acquainted with such companions."

Black Will knew many criminals.

"What manner of man was he?" Black Will asked.

Bradshaw described the man: "A lean-faced writhen — twisted in his body — knave, hawk-nosed and very hollow-eyed, with mighty furrows in his stormy brows; long hair curled down his shoulders. His chin was bare with no beard, but on his upper lip was a mustachio, which he wound about his ear."

"What apparel had he?" Black Will asked. "What was he wearing?"

Bradshaw said:

"A watchet satin doublet all torn; the inner side did bear the greater show."

In other words: He was wearing a light-blue jacket so completely torn up that people could see more of the lining of the jacket than they could see of its outside layer.

Bradshaw continued:

"A pair of thread-bare velvet breeches, with torn seams, a worsted-wool stocking torn above the shoe, a livery — a servant's — cloak, but all the lace was off; it was bad, but yet it served to hide the plate."

We can ask this: If he was the servant of Sir Antony Cooke, why was his clothing so torn up?

Black Will said, "Sirrah Shakebag, can thou remember when we trolled — passed around — the drinking bowl at the town of Sittingburgh, where I broke the head of the tapster of the Lion Tavern with a cudgel-stick?"

A tapster is a bartender.

A broken head is a bleeding head.

"Aye, very well, Black Will," Shakebag said.

Black Will said:

"Why, it was with the money that the plate was sold for."

This sounds very much like Black Will was one of the people who stole the plate.

He then asked:

"Sirrah Bradshaw, what will thou give him who can tell thee who sold thy plate?"

"Who, I ask thee, good Will?" Bradshaw asked.

"Why, it was one Jack Fitten," Black Will said. "He's now in Newgate Prison for stealing a horse, and he shall be arraigned — charged for the crime — the next assize."

A "fitten" is 1) a lie, and/or 2) an invention.

Black Will may be lying to Bradshaw.

Bradshaw said:

"Why, then let Lord Cheiny seek Jack Fitten forth, for I'll go back and tell him who robbed him of his plate. This cheers my heart."

He then said:

"Master Greene, I'll leave you, for I must speedily go to the Isle of Sheppy."

The Lord Cheiny lived on the Isle of Sheppy.

Dick Greene said, "Before you go, let me entreat you to carry this letter to Mistress Arden of Faversham and humbly recommend me to herself — humbly remember me to her."

Bradshaw said:

"That will I, Master Greene, and so farewell.

"Here, Will, there's a crown for thy good news."

He gave him a coin.

Bradshaw exited.

Black Will said:

"Farewell, Bradshaw; I'll drink no water for thy sake while this lasts."

The crown would be spent on alcohol.

He said to Dick Greene:

"Now, gentleman, shall we have your company as we go to London?"

Dick Greene said, "Nay, stay, wait, sirs. A little more I must use your help, and in a matter of great consequence, wherein if you'll be secret and profound — that is, cunning and crafty — I'll give you twenty angels for your pains."

Angels are gold coins.

"What! Twenty angels? Give my fellow George Shakebag and me twenty angels?" Black Will said. "And if thou shall have thy own father slain, so that thou may inherit his land, we'll kill him."

"Aye, thy mother, thy sister, thy brother, or all thy kin," Shakebag said.

Dick Greene said:

"Well, this it is: Arden of Faversham has highly wronged me about the Abbey land, so that no revenge but death will serve the turn and meet the situation.

"Will you two kill him? Here's the angels as a down payment, and I will lay the platform of his death — I will make up a plan for killing Arden."

He showed them the money.

Black Will said, "Plat me no platforms; give me the money, and I'll stab him as he stands pissing against a wall, but I'll kill him."

"Where is he?" Shakebag asked.

"He is now at London, in Aldersgate Street," Dick Greene said.

"He's as dead as if he had been condemned by an Act of Parliament, if once Black Will and I swear his death," Shakebag said.

"Here are ten pounds, and when he is dead, ye shall have twenty more," Dick Greene said.

Greene handed over the ten pounds.

Black Will said:

"My fingers itch to be at the peasant. Ah, that I might be set to work thus through the year, and that murder would grow to become such an occupation that a man might follow it without danger of law.

"By God's wounds, I warrant I would be warden of the company of murderers!"

Terry Pratchett's Discworld series has a guild of murderers; the Patrician, a dictator, got his training there. In real life, Vladimir Putin may be regarded as the head of such a guild.

Black Will said to Dick Greene:

"Come, let us be going, and we'll bait — eat — in Rochester, where I'll give thee a gallon of sack — white wine — to handsel and confirm the match and seal the deal with."

As a noun, a handsel is a gift given as a token of good luck.

— 2.2 —

Scene 3

In London, standing on a street near St. Paul's, Michael said to himself:

"I have gotten such a letter as will touch and upset the painter."

Michael had stated earlier that he would get someone to write a letter for him. Or perhaps he had begotten — written — his own letter.

Both Michael and Clarke wanted to marry Susan, Mosbie's sister.

Michael said to himself, "And thus it is."

Arden and Franklin entered the scene. Unnoticed by Michael, they heard him read his letter.

Michael read out loud:

"My duty remembered, Mistress Susan, hoping in God that you are in good health, as I Michael was at the making hereof. This is to certify and inform you that as the turtledove true and faithful, when she has lost her mate, sits alone, so I, mourning for your absence, do walk up and down St. Paul's courtyard until one day I fell asleep and lost my master's pantofles."

"Pantofles" are outdoor overshoes. Arden had been inside the church while Michael waited outside. Much business was conducted in the central aisle of St. Paul's Cathedral. Some theft occurred in the churchyard.

Michael continued reading the letter out loud:

"Ah, Mistress Susan, abolish and rid yourself of that paltry painter, cut him off at the shins with a frowning look of your crabbed countenance, and think upon Michael, who, drunk with the dregs of your favor, will cleave as fast and securely to your love as a plaster of pitch — a medicinal substance — to a galled and blistered horse-back.

"Thus hoping you will let my passions penetrate, or rather impetrate — obtain by asking for — mercy at your meek hands, I end.

"Yours, Michael, or else not Michael."

Michael was not educated in rhetoric. Striving to achieve alliteration, he wrote that Susan had a "crabbed countenance," which means "disagreeable face." Also, he referred to the "dregs" of her favor. "Dregs" are bits of solids at the bottom of a glass of wine.

33

Arden said to Michael, "Why, you paltry, worthless knave, do you stand here loitering, knowing the importance of my business affairs, and what haste my business needs to send word to Kent?"

Arden, of course, wanted to finish his business in London quickly in order to return home to Kent.

"Indeed, friend Michael, this is very ill because you know that your master has no other serving-man than you with him," Franklin said. "Do you slack in carrying out his business so you can carry out your own?"

Arden said:

"Where is the letter, sirrah? Let me see it."

Michael had tried to hide the letter when he learned of Arden and Franklin's presence, but now he handed over the letter.

In this society, masters had much power, and servants had few rights.

Arden continued:

"See, Master Franklin, here's proper stuff: Susan my maid, the painter, and my serving-man, a crew of harlots, male and female, are all in love, truly."

He then said to Michael:

"Sirrah, let me hear no more about this, nor for thy life — on pain of death — shall thou once write to her a word."

Dick Greene, Black Will, and Shakebag entered the scene.

Arden continued:

"Will thou be married to so base a trull — so base a whore? She is Mosbie's sister. Once I come home, I'll rouse her from remaining in my house: I will remove her from my house.

"Now, Master Franklin, let us go walk inside St. Paul's. Come but a turn or two, and then let's go away."

St. Paul's was a good place to talk and to meet people.

Arden, Franklin, and Michael exited.

"The first man is Arden, and that's his serving-man," Dick Greene said. "The other man is Franklin, Arden's dearest friend."

"By God's wounds, I'll kill all three of them," Black Will said.

Dick Greene said:

"Nay, sirs, don't touch his serving-man for any reason, but stand hidden nearby, and take the best standing place from which to ambush him, and at his coming forth send him speedily to his death."

Dick Greene then said to himself: "To the Nag's Head Tavern, there is this coward's haunt."

He was calling himself a coward: He did not want to actively participate in the murder, and so he would go to an inn.

He had a reputation for being religious.

He then said out loud:

"But now I'll leave you until the deed is done."

Shakebag said, "If Arden should not be paid his own and given what he deserves, never trust Shakebag."

Dick Greene exited.

Black Will said, "Sirrah Shakebag, at his coming forth I'll run him through with a dagger, and then we shall go to the Blackfriars, and there take to water in a boat and get away."

"Why, that's the best plan," Shakebag said, "but make sure that thou don't miss him."

"How can I miss him, when I think about the forty more angels I must have if I don't miss him?" Black Will said.

At this time, an angel was worth one-half British pound.

An apprentice entered the scene and said, "It is very late; I would do best to shut up my book stall, for here will be old filching — the customary shoplifting, when the crowd comes out of Saint Paul's."

He let down the shutter of his stall. It hit Black Will's head and caused it to bleed.

"By God's wounds, draw your sword, Shakebag, draw, I am almost killed," Black Will said.

The apprentice, who was not intimidated, said, "We'll attame — attack — you, I warrant."

If Black Will and Shakebag fought him, the apprentice promised that he — with help from other apprentices — would fight back.

Apprentices were not afraid to brawl. If an apprentice shouted "Clubs! Clubs!" lots of other apprentices would instantly appear and be ready to fight in support of whichever apprentice needed help.

People were watching the argument, and some of those people were likely apprentices.

Aware of the danger of the apprentices, Black Will said, "By God's wounds, I am tame enough already."

Arden, Franklin, and Michael entered the scene.

"What troublesome fray or mutiny — that is, tumult — is this?" Arden asked.

Franklin said, "It is nothing but some brabbling, noisy, paltry fray, devised to pick men's pockets in the throng."

Franklin thought that it was an orchestrated fight designed to distract bystanders so that their pockets could be picked.

"Is that all it is?" Arden said. "Come, Franklin, let's go away."

Arden, Franklin, and Michael exited.

"What amends shall I have for my broken head?" Black Will asked the apprentice.

"By the Virgin Mary, this amends, that if you don't get yourselves away all the sooner, you shall be well beaten and sent to the Counter," the apprentice said.

The Counter was a prison.

The apprentice exited.

Black Will said:

"Well, I'll be gone, but look after the signs of your shop, for I'll pull them down all.

"Shakebag, my broken — my bleeding — head does not grieve me as much as that by this means Arden has escaped.

"I had a glimpse of him and his companion."

Dick Greene entered the scene and said:

"Why, sirs, Arden's as well as I am; I met him and Franklin going merrily to the ordinary."

An ordinary is an inn that served meals.

Greene continued:

"What! Don't you dare to kill him?"

Black Will said:

"Yes, sir, we dare do it; but, if we two and you were to go back in time and make the agreement again, we would not do it for less than ten pounds more. I value every drop of my blood at a French crown."

A French crown is a gold coin, and it is baldness caused by the "French disease": syphilis.

Black Will continued:

"I have had ten pounds to steal a dog, and we have no more here to kill a man; but except that a bargain is a bargain, and so forth, you should do it yourself."

"And so forth" means "yadda, yadda": You know the rest.

"I ask thee, how came thy head to be bleeding?" Dick Greene said.

"Why, thou see it is bleeding, don't thou?" Black Will said.

In other words: *How* it came to be bleeding is not important.

Shakebag said:

"We were standing against a stall, watching for Arden's coming, when a boy let down his shop-window and broke Black Will's head; whereupon arose a brawl, and in the tumult, Arden escaped us and passed by unthought on — we had forgotten about him.

"But forbearance is no acquittance; another time we'll do it, I promise thee."

In other words: Although they would let Arden live for the time being, he would in fact die soon. Acquittance of the contract to murder Arden would be postponed, but it would in fact happen.

Dick Greene said:

"I ask thee, Will, to make clean thy bloody brow, and let us think about some other place where Arden may be met with handsomely and conveniently for our purpose.

"Remember how devoutly thou have sworn to kill the villain; think upon thine oath."

Black Will had sworn to kill Arden.

Black Will said:

"Bah, I have broken five hundred oaths!

"But if thou would charm and bewitch me to effect this deed, tell me about gold, my resolution's fee."

In other words: If you want to motivate me to kill Arden, tell me about the money I will make by killing him.

Black Will continued:

"Say that thou see Mosbie kneeling at my knees, offering me service for my high attempt — my worthy deed. And say that thou see sweet Alice Arden, with a lap full of crowns — gold coins — coming with a lowly curtsey to the earth, saying 'Take this but for thy quarterage — thy quarterly payment. Such yearly tribute will I answer — give and guarantee — thee.'

"Why, this would steel soft-mettled cowardice, with which Black Will was never tainted yet."

Black Will wanted more than money: He wanted a certain amount of deference from Mosbie and Alice.

He continued:

"I tell thee, Greene, that even the forlorn, lost traveler, whose lips are glued and stuck together with summer's parching heat, never longed so much to see a running brook as I long to finish Arden's tragedy.

"See thou this gore that cleaves to my face? From hence I will never wash this bloody stain until Arden's heart is panting — is beating — in my hand."

"Why, that's well said," Dick Greene said, "but what does Shakebag say?"

"I cannot paint my valor — describe my bravery — with words," Shakebag said, "but, if thou give me place and opportunity, such mercy as the starved lioness, when she is sucked dry by her eager young, shows to the prey that next encounters her, I would take on Arden so much pity."

Dick Greene said:

"So should it fare with men of firm resolve.

"And now, sirs, seeing that this accident of meeting him in St. Paul's has no success, let us think about some other place whose earth may swallow up this Arden's blood."

Michael, Arden's serving-man, entered the scene.

Seeing him, Dick Greene said:

"See, yonder comes his serving-man, and do you know what? The foolish knave is in love with Mosbie's sister, and for her sake, whose love he cannot get unless Mosbie solicits — that is, pleads — his suit, the villain has sworn the slaughter of his master."

In other words: Michael cannot get Susan as his wife unless her brother, Mosbie, intercedes for him. To get that help from Mosbie, Michael was willing to kill Arden.

Dick Greene continued:

"We'll question him, for he may help us and give us much information.

"How are you now, Michael, and where are you going?"

"My master has just now eaten, and I am going to prepare his chamber for sleeping," Michael said.

"Where did Master Arden eat?" Dick Greene asked.

Michael answered:

"At the Nag's Head, at the eighteen-pence ordinary."

A meal could be purchased for eighteen pence at this inn that serves meals.

Recognizing the people with Dick Greene, Michael said:

"How are you now, Master Shakebag?

"What! Black Will! By God's dear lady, how does it chance — how does it happen — that your face is so bloody?"

"Bah, sirrah, there is a chance in it — it was bad luck," Black Will said. "This sauciness in you will make you be knocked and beaten."

"Nay, if you are offended, I'll be gone," Michael said.

"Stay, Michael, you may not escape us so," Dick Greene said. "Michael, I know you love your master well."

Michael's master was Arden, whom Michael wanted to kill.

"Why, so I do," Michael said, "but why do you mention that?"

"Because I think you love your mistress better," Dick Greene said.

Michael's "mistress" can be his female boss (Alice), or it can be his loved one (Susan).

Thinking of Alice, Michael said, "I do not think that; but tell me, truly, what if I should?"

Shakebag said to Dick Greene:

"Come to the purpose; come to the point."

Shakebag then said:

"Michael, we hear that you have a pretty love in Faversham."

"Why, I have two or three! What's that to thee!" Michael said.

Black Will said to Shakebag:

"You deal too mildly with the peasant."

He then said to Michael:

"Thus it is:

"It is known to us that you love Mosbie's sister. We know besides that you have taken your oath to further Mosbie and assist him to enjoy your mistress' — Alice's — bed and to kill your master for his sister's sake.

"Now, sir, a poorer coward than yourself was never fostered and raised in the coast of Kent. How does it happen then that such a knave as you dare to swear to perform a matter of such consequence?"

"Ah, Will," Dick Greene said.

Black Will was giving Michael much delicate information.

Black Will said to Greene:

"Bah, give me permission to speak."

He then said to Michael:

"There's no more but this: Since thou have sworn to murder your master, we dare to discover all — to reveal everything.

"And in case thou had or should thou utter and reveal what I will tell thee, we have devised an underhand plot that no matter what shall happen to any of us, we will send thee roundly — directly — to the devil of hell. We will kill thee.

"And therefore this is what I reveal to thee: I am the very man, marked in my birth-hour by the Destinies to put an end to Arden's life on earth."

The Destinies are the Fates.

Black Will was saying that he was fated to murder Arden.

Black Will continued:

"Thou are only a member — a helper and assistant — who will just whet the knife whose edge must search the closet of his breast."

In other words: Michael will metaphorically sharpen the knife that will be stuck in Arden's heart.

Black Will continued:

"Thy office — responsibility — is just to appoint the place and lure thy master to his tragedy. My office — my responsibility — is to perform it when the occasion arises.

"So then don't be squeamish, but here plan with us how and in what way we may conclude and bring about Arden's death."

"So shall thou purchase — acquire — Mosbie for thy friend: Thou shall earn Mosbie's favor by doing this," Shakebag said. "And by his friendship thou shall gain his sister's love."

"So shall thy mistress be thy favorer: Alice shall help persuade Mosbie's sister to marry thee," Dick Greene said. "And thou shall be disburdened of the oath thou made: Thou need not be the one who shall murder Arden."

Michael said:

"Well, gentlemen, I cannot do otherwise than confess, since you have urged me so apparently and plainly, that I have vowed my master Arden's death, and Arden, whose kindly love and liberal, generous hand deserves nothing but good service from me, I will deliver over to your hands.

"Tonight, go to his house on Aldersgate Street. The doors I'll leave unlocked in anticipation of your coming. No sooner shall you enter through the latched door, over the threshold to the inner courtyard of the house, than on your left hand you shall see the stairs that lead directly to my master's bedchamber: There you shall find him and dispose of him as you please.

"Now it would be good for us to part company. What I have promised, I will perform."

"If you should deceive us, it would go badly with you," Black Will said.

"I will accomplish all I have revealed," Michael said.

"Come, let's go drink," Black Will said. "Choler and anger make me as dry as a dog."

Black Will, Dick Greene, and Shakebag exited.

Michael remained behind.

Alone, he said to himself:

"Thus the lamb feeling safe grazes on the hill, while through the thicket of a wood the hunger-bitten wolf looks over its territory and takes advantage to eat the lamb.

"Ah, harmless, innocent Arden, how have thou transgressed, thou whom thus thy gentle life is aimed at?

"Many good deeds thou have done for me. Now I must pay thee back by betraying thee, although I am a man who should take the weapon in my hand and buckler — and shield — thee from ill-intending foes.

"I, unsuspected by thee, do lead thee with a wicked deceitful smile to the slaughter-house. So I have sworn to Mosbie and my mistress, and so I have promised to the slaughtermen.

"And if I should not deal genuinely with them, their lawless rage would take revenge on me.

"Bah, I will spurn at — kick against — mercy for this once.
"Let pity lodge and reside where feeble women lie.
"I am resolved, and Arden must necessarily die."

CHAPTER 3
— 3.1 —
Scene 4

Arden and Franklin spoke together in a room in Franklin's house on Aldersgate Street in London. Arden was depressed and pessimistic about his wife, Alice.

Arden said:

"No, Franklin, no.

"If fear or stormy threats, if love of me or the caring of womanhood, if fear of God or the common speech — the common gossip — of men, who mangle reputation with their wounding words, and couch dishonor as dishonor buds, might enjoin — might impose — repentance in her wanton, lustful thoughts, then there would be no doubt that she would turn over a new leaf and feel sorrow for her dissolute, immoral life.

"Once dishonor starts, gossips nourish it and make it grow by ruining reputations."

According to the *Oxford English Dictionary*, "to couch" means "To lay, set, bed (plants or slips) in the earth."

Arden continued:

"But she is rooted in her wickedness, perverse and stubborn, not to be reclaimed: not to be won back by me or reformed.

"Good counsel is to her as rain to weeds, and reprehension — criticism — makes her vice grow just like a Hydra's head that is replenished by its destruction."

Hercules' second labor was killing the Lernaean Hydra. In accomplishing this labor, Heracles had the help of a nephew named Iolaus. The Hydra of Lerna was a monstrous snake that had nine heads, the middle of which was immortal. Heracles and Iolaus traveled to Lerna and found the Hydra's lair. Heracles forced the Hydra to leave its lair by shooting flaming arrows into the lair. Hercules fought the Hydra, but he discovered that each time a mortal head was cut off, two more heads grew in its place. Therefore, each time Hercules cut off one of the Hydra's mortal heads, Iolaus cauterized it with a torch, thus preventing more heads from growing. Hercules then cut off the immortal head and placed it under a boulder.

Arden continued:

"Her faults, I think, are painted in my face, for every searching eye to read over; and Mosbie's name, a scandal to mine, is deeply trenched and engraved in my blushing brow.

"Ah, Franklin, Franklin, when I think about this, my heart's grief tears away my other powers worse than the spiritual conflict at the hour of death."

Franklin said:

"Gentle Arden, stop this sad lament: She will amend and improve her behavior, and so your griefs will cease. Or else she'll die, and so your sorrows will end.

If neither of these two does haply — happily or happen to — befall, yet let your comfort be that others bear your woes, twice doubled all, with patience."

"My house is irksome and loathsome," Arden said. "There I cannot rest."

"Then stay with me in London," Franklin said. "Don't go home."

Arden said:

"Then that base Mosbie usurps my room — my space — and makes his triumph from my being away from home."

The room, aka space, is Alice's vagina.

Arden put his hand over his heart and said:

"At home or not at home, wherever I am, here, here pain lies, ah, Franklin, here pain lies that will not go out of my heart until wretched Arden dies."

Michael, Arden's man-servant, entered the scene.

"Forget your griefs a while," Franklin said. "Here comes your serving-man."

"What time is it, sirrah?" Arden asked.

"Almost ten," Michael said.

Arden said:

"See! See! How quickly passes the wearisome time!

"Come, Master Franklin, shall we go to bed?"

In this society, two people of the same sex could share a bed together without negative comment. Doing so prevented loneliness and provided warmth in cold weather.

Franklin said, "Please, go ahead of me. I'll follow you."

Arden and Michael exited.

Alone, Franklin said to himself:

"Ah, what a hell is fretful jealousy!

"What pity-moving words, what heavy sighs, what grievous groans and overburdening woes and troubles accompany this gentle gentleman!

"One moment he shakes his oppressed-by-worries head, and then his sad eyes fix on the sullen earth, ashamed to appear in public and gaze upon the open, public world.

"The next moment he casts his eyes up towards the heavens, looking that way for redress of wrong.

"Sometimes he seeks to beguile his grief and tells a story with his anxious tongue. Then comes his wife's dishonor in his thoughts and he cuts off his tale in the middle, pouring fresh sorrow on his weary limbs.

"So woe-begone, so internally filled with woe ...

"There was never anyone who lived and bore it so."

Michael returned and said, "My master wants you to come to bed."

"Is he himself already in his bed?" Franklin asked.

"He is, and he would like to have the light taken away," Michael said.

Franklin exited.

Alone, Michael considered his options: 1) to help in the plot to kill Arden, or 2) to reveal the plot to Arden.

He said to himself:

"Conflicting thoughts, camped in my breast, awaken me with the echo of their strokes, and I, a judge to pronounce judgment for either side, can give to neither wished-for victory."

Michael wanted to know definitely and without doubt what he should do. But he could not decide what to do.

He continued saying to himself:

"My master's kindness pleads to me for life with just demand, and I must grant it to him.

"My mistress, Alice, has forced me to make an oath, for Susan's sake, the which I may not break, for that is nearer to my heart than a master's love.

"That grim-faced fellow, pitiless Black Will, and Shakebag, stern in bloody stratagem — two rougher ruffians never lived in Kent — have sworn my death if I infringe my vow and break my promise to help them, a dreadful thing to consider."

Pretending that he was speaking to Arden, Michael said:

"I think I see them with their bolstered — bristly — hair staring and grinning in thy gentle face, and in their ruthless hands their daggers drawn, exulting over thee with a heap of oaths, while thou, submissive and pleading for relief, are mangled by their ireful — furious — instruments.

"I think I hear them ask where Michael is, and pitiless Black Will cries, 'Stab the slave! The peasant will expose the tragedy — Arden's murder!'

"The wrinkles in Black Will's foul death-threatening face gapes open wide, like graves gape to swallow men.

"My death to him is but a merriment, and he will murder me to amuse himself."

Michael then shouted:

"He comes! He comes! Ah, Master Franklin, help! Call on the neighbors, or we are but dead!"

Franklin and Arden came running.

"What dismal outcry calls me from my rest?" Franklin asked.

"What has caused such a fearful cry?" Arden said. "Speak, Michael. Has anything injured thee?"

Michael said:

"Nothing, sir, but as I fell asleep, upon the threshold leaning against the stairs, I had a fearful dream that troubled me, and in my slumber, I thought I was beset with murderer-thieves who came to rifle — rob — me. My trembling joints are evidence of my inward fear.

"I beg your pardons for disturbing you."

"So great a cry for nothing I never heard," Arden said. "What! Are the doors fast locked and all things safe?"

"I cannot tell," Michael said. "I think I locked the doors."

Arden said:

"I don't like this, but I'll go see myself."

He checked the locks and then returned and said to Michael:

"Never trust me again if I am lying, but the doors were all unlocked. This negligence contents me not half: It displeases me.

"Go to bed, and if you love my favor and want to stay on my good side, let me have no more such pranks and foolish acts as these."

He then said:

"Come, Master Franklin, let us go to bed."
Franklin said:
"Aye, by my faith; the air is very cold.
"Michael, farewell; I hope that thou dream no more."

— 3.2 —

Scene 5

Will, Dick Greene, and Shakebag spoke together outside Franklin's house.

Shakebag said:

"Black night has hidden the pleasures of the day, and sheeting — enveloping and covering — darkness overhangs the earth, and with the black fold of her cloudy robe, black night obscures us from the eyesight of the world, in which sweet silence such as we triumph and prevail."

Night is when criminals such as Black Will and Shakebag make much of their money.

Shakebag continued:

"The lazy minutes linger on their time and pass slowly, as loath to give due audit and proper reckoning to the hour, until in the watch — the watching in the night — our purpose is complete, and Arden has been sent to the everlasting night that is death.

"Greene, leave, and linger here nearby, and at some hour from now come to us again, where we will give you evidence of his death."

"May my wish be successful, despite whosoever will say no to it," Dick Greene said, "and so I'll leave you for an hour or two."

He exited.

Black Will said:

"I tell thee, Shakebag, I wish that this thing was done. I am so heavy that I can scarcely walk."

"Heavy" can mean 1) sleepy, and 2) distressed.

Black Will continued:

"This drowsiness in me bodes little good."

"Drowsiness" can mean 1) sleepiness, and 2) lethargy.

Shakebag said:

"How are thou now, Will? Will thou become a precisian?"

Puritans are precisians: sanctimonious believers.

Shakebag continued:

48

"If so, then let's go sleep. We might as well when bugbears and fears shall kill our courage with their fancy's — their imagination's — work."

Black Will said:

"Why, Shakebag, thou mistake me much, and thou wrong me, too, in telling me about fear and accusing me of being afraid.

"If it weren't a serious thing we go about, the murder of Arden should be put off until I had fought with thee, to let thee know I am no coward, I.

"I tell thee, Shakebag, thou abuse and wrong me."

"Why, thy speech betrayed an inly-kind of — an inward — fear and savored — reeked — of a weak-relenting spirit," Shakebag said. "Go forward and continue now in that which we have begun, and afterwards attack me when thou dare."

"And if I do not, may Heaven cut off my life!" Black Will said. "But let that pass and show me to this house where Arden is staying. There thou shall see I'll do as much as Shakebag."

"This is the door — but wait, I think it is locked," Shakebag said. "The villain Michael has deceived us."

Black Will said:

"Wait, let me see, Shakebag."

He tried the door and then said:

"It's locked indeed. Knock with thy sword, perhaps the slave will hear."

Shakebag's social status was not that of a gentleman, and so by law he ought not to be carrying a sword. For gentlemen, the sword was an identifier of social status; for Shakebag, it was a tool of his trade — murder.

"What we planned will not be. The white-livered — cowardly — peasant has gone to bed, and he laughs us both to scorn," Shakebag said. "He mocks us by laughing at us."

Black Will said:

"And he shall buy his merriment as dear as ever coistril bought so little sport."

A coistril is a custrel: a knave or rogue.

Black Will swore:

"Never let this sword assist me when I need, but let it rust and canker — rust and corrode — after I have sworn, if I, the next time that I meet the hind, don't lop away his leg, his arm, or both."

A "hind" is a servant. Black Will was referring to Michael.

Shakebag swore, "And let me never draw a sword again, nor prosper in the twilight, cockshut light, when I would fleece and rob the wealthy traveler, but instead let me lie and languish in a loathsome den, hated and spit at by the passersby, and in that death may I die unpitied, if I, the next time that I meet the slave, don't cut off the nose from the coward's face and trample on it for this villainy."

The cockshut light is twilight. It is when poultry roosts: when cocks, hens, and chicks are shut up for the night.

"Come, let's go and seek Dick Greene," Black Will said. "I know he'll swear and be upset."

Shakebag said, "He would be a villain, if he would not swear. It would make a peasant swear among his boys, who never dared say anything before but 'yea' and 'no,' to be thus flouted of a coistril — to be thus mocked by a villain."

The peasant is a father who is trying to bring up his boys to be respectful and to not use swear words or to swear unnecessary and unethical oaths.

Black Will said, "Shakebag, let's seek out Greene, and in the morning at the alehouse abutting on Arden's house let's watch the out-coming of that prick-eared cur — that pointed-eared dog, and then leave it to me alone to handle him."

The "prick-eared cur" was Michael, who had not kept his word: He had not left the door unlocked.

— 3.3 —

Scene 6

The next morning, Arden, Franklin, and Michael stood together in a room in Franklin's house.

Arden ordered Michael:

"Sirrah, go to Billingsgate Wharf and learn what time the tide will serve our purposes."

It was best to row with — not against — the tide.

Arden continued:

"Come to us in St. Paul's.

"First go make the bed, and afterwards go ask about the flood tide."

Michael exited.

Arden then said:

"Come, Master Franklin, you shall go with me. This night I dreamed that being in a park, a toil was pitched to overthrow the deer."

In other words: A large net or a series of nets were set up to bring down the deer. Dogs and servants would drive the deer into the nets.

Arden continued describing his dream:

"And I upon a little rising hill stood whistly watching — silently watching — for the herd's approach. Even there, I thought, a gentle slumber took me, and summoned all my parts to sweet repose.

"But in the pleasure of this golden rest an ill-thewed — an ill-mannered — forester had removed the net and had surrounded me with that beguiling home — the net — which recently, I thought, was pitched to bring down the deer.

"With that he blew an evil-sounding hunting-horn, and at the noise another herdsman came, with fauchon — a curved sword — drawn, and pointed it at my breast, crying aloud, 'Thou are the game we seek!'

"With this I awakened and trembled in every joint, like a person obscured and hidden in a little bush, who sees a lion foraging about, and when the dreadful forest-king the lion is gone, the hidden person peers about with fearful suspicion through the thorny gaps — the 'windows' — in the thicket, and he

51

will not think his person free from danger, but quakes and shivers, although the cause of his fear has gone."

Having finished describing his dream, Arden said:

"So, trust me, Franklin, when I did awake, I stood in doubt whether or not I was really awake. This fond — foolish — unexpected dream made such a great impression on me.

"May God grant that this vision bedeem — decree — me any good: May God grant that this is a good omen and not a bad omen."

The prefix "be-" is an intensifier of the root word: "deem."

"This fantasy does rise from Michael's fear. Michael, being awakened with the noise he made, his troubled senses yet could take no rest," Franklin said. "And this, I assure you, produced your dream."

"It may be so," Arden said. "May God cause it to turn out for the best, but often my dreams truly foretell the future."

"To such as note their nightly fantasies — that is, remember their dreams — perhaps one in twenty may incur belief," Franklin said. "But don't treat your dream like that; your dream is only a mockery: It is something to be mocked."

Arden said:

"Come, Master Franklin; we'll now walk in St. Paul's and dine together at the ordinary, and at the time my serving-man tells us is the best time to take to water, we will withdraw to the wharf, and with the tide go down to Faversham.

"Tell me, Master Franklin, shall it not be so?"

"At your good pleasure, sir," Franklin said. "As you wish. I'll bear you company."

— 3.4 —

Scene 7

Black Will, Dick Greene, and Shakebag saw Michael at Aldersgate.

"Draw your sword, Shakebag, for here's that villain Michael," Black Will said.

"First, Will, let's hear what he can say," Dick Greene said.

Black Will said to Michael, "Speak, milksop slave, and never afterward speak because you will be dead."

A "milksop" is a coward.

Black Will was threatening to kill Michael.

Michael said:

"For God's sake, sirs, let me excuse myself. For here I swear, by Heaven and earth and all, I did perform my task to the utmost, and I left the doors unbolted and unlocked.

"But see the chance occurrence: Franklin and my master were very late conferring in the porch, and Franklin left his handkerchief where he sat with some gold tied up in it, as he said.

"Being in bed, he remembered the gold, and coming down to get it, he found the doors unlocked. He locked the gates, and brought away the keys, for which offence — leaving the gates unlocked — my master berated me.

"But now I am going to see the state of the tide, for with a good tide my master will leave London, where you may confront him well on Rainham Down, a place well-fitting such a stratagem as yours."

Black Will said:

"Your excuse has somewhat mollified my choler and anger.

"Why now, Greene, it is better now than ever it was."

"But, Michael, is this true?" Dick Greene asked.

"As true as I report it to be true," Michael said.

"Then, Michael, this shall be your penance, to feast us all at the Salutation Inn, where we will plan the attainment of our goal thoroughly," Shakebag said.

Dick Greene said, "And, Michael, you shall bear no news of this tide because these two may be in Rainham Down before your master."

53

Dick Greene wanted Black Will and Shakebag to arrive at Rainham Down before Arden and Franklin, and so he did not want Michael to take news about the tide back to Arden. That would slow down Arden and Franklin.

"Why, I'll agree to anything you'll have me, as long as you will accept my company," Michael said.

They were forcing Michael to go with them to the Salutation Tavern — and to pay the bill. Michael was too afraid of them to say no.

— 3.5 —

Scene 8

Alone in a room in Arden's house at Faversham, Mosbie said to himself:

"Disturbed thoughts drive me away from company and dry my marrow — my courage and spirit — with their watchfulness and wakefulness.

"Continual trouble of my moody brain enfeebles my body by excess of drink and nips me as the bitter north-east wind checks the tender blossoms in the spring."

He was metaphorically drinking troubles, and/or he was literally drinking too much alcohol because of his troubles.

Mosbie continued saying to himself:

"Well fares the man, however his cates — his food — tastes, who eats at a table without foul suspicion, fears, and anxieties. In contrast, a man whose troubled mind is stuffed with discontent only pines and wastes away among his delicates — his favorite foods.

"My golden time was when I had no gold. Although then I lacked wealth, yet I slept secure. My daily toil and work begat night's rest and repose for me. My night's rest and repose made daylight fresh to me.

"But since I climbed the top-bough of the tree and sought to build my nest among the clouds, each gentle starry gale shakes my bed, and makes me dread my downfall to the earth."

In other words: Every gentle breeze makes him feel that he will fall to the ground.

A "gentle gale" is an oxymoron, as gales are very strong winds. To Mosbie, because of his troubles, even a gentle wind feels like a gale.

A "starry gale" is a high wind, as if among the stars.

Mosbie continued saying to himself:

"But whither does contemplation carry me? Where does thinking about this reflection take me?

"The way I seek to find, where pleasure dwells, is hedged behind me so that I cannot go back, but I necessarily must go on, although to danger's gate."

In other words: I must follow the path that I am on, although it may lead to danger.

Mosbie continued saying to himself:

"So then, Arden, perish thou by that decree and decision. For Greene ears — plows — the land and weeds thee up to make my harvest nothing but pure corn.

"And for his pains I'll heave him up and extol him for a while, and afterward I'll smother him to have his wax. Such bees as Greene must never live to sting."

Beekeepers used smoke to calm bees so the beekeepers could remove the bees' wax and honey.

Dick Greene was doing Mosbie's dirty work: He was arranging the murder of Arden, a murder from which Mosbie would financially benefit. Mosbie would let him do that, and then he would find a way to kill Greene or have him killed.

Mosbie continued saying to himself:

"Then there are Michael and the painter, too, chief actors to Arden's overthrow and destruction. When they shall see me sit in Arden's seat — home — they will insult me for my meed — my reward, or they will frighten me by threatening to reveal how Arden died.

"I'll have none of that, for I can cast a bone to make these curs pluck out each other's throat, and then I am the sole ruler of my own."

Mosbie was planning to have Michael the serving-man and Clarke the painter fight over Susan.

Mosbie continued saying to himself:

"Yet Mistress Arden lives, but she's myself, and holy Church rites makes us two but one."

After Arden was dead, Mosbie planned to legally marry Alice, who was like himself. Both were unworthy of trust.

Mosbie continued saying to himself:

"But so what? I may not trust you, Alice. You have supplanted Arden for my sake, and you will extirpate — will root up — me to plant another. It is terrifying sleeping in a serpent's bed, and I will completely rid my hands of her."

Alice, holding a prayerbook, entered the scene.

Seeing her, Mosbie said to himself:

"But here she comes, and I must flatter her and be nice to her."

He said out loud:

"How are thou now, Alice? What! Sad and emotional? Make me partaker of thy sorrow and pensiveness: Fire divided burns with lesser force."

In other words: Share your cares and concerns with me, and they will hurt you less.

Alice said:

"But I will dam that fire in my breast until by the force thereof my part consume."

She wanted to suppress her passion until it consumed itself and died.

Alice then sighed and said:

"Ah, Mosbie!"

Mosbie said:

"Such deep pathaires — outbursts of emotion — which are like a cannon's burst discharged against a ruined wall, break my relenting heart in a thousand pieces.

"Ungentle, unkind Alice, thy sorrow is my sore. Thou know it well, and it is thy policy to forge and fashion distressful looks to wound a breast where lies a heart that dies when thou are sad. It is not love that loves to anger love."

"It is not love that loves to murder love," Alice said.

"What do you mean by that?" Mosbie asked.

"Thou know how dearly Arden loved me," Alice said.

"And what about it then?" Mosbie asked.

Alice said:

"And then — I shall conceal the rest, for it is too bad to speak, lest my words be carried with the wind, and proclaimed in and known to the world to both our shames.

"I ask thee, Mosbie, to let our springtime wither; our harvest else will yield but loathsome weeds."

Their springtime was their love, which was still young.

Alice continued:

"Forget, I ask thee, what has passed between us, for now I blush and tremble at the thoughts!"

"What!" Mosbie said. "Have you changed?"

Alice said:

"Aye, to my former happy life again, from the title of an odious strumpet's — an odious whore's — name to honest Arden's wife, although not Arden's honest — chaste — wife.

"Ha, Mosbie! It is thou who has rifled and robbed me of that former happy life and made me slanderous to all my kin. Even in my forehead is thy name engraved, a mean artificer — a low-born craftsman — that low-born name.

"I was bewitched: Woe worth — a curse upon — the hapless, unfortunate hour and all the causes and reasons that enchanted me!"

Mosbie said:

"Nay, if thou ban and curse me, let me breathe curses forth, and if you stand so nicely and insist so fastidiously on your fame and reputation, let me repent the credit and good name that I have lost.

"I have neglected matters of importance that would have stated me above thy state — that would have raised my social position above your social position.

"I have forslowed and not taken advantage of my opportunities, and I have spurned at — wasted — time.

"Aye, Mosbie has forsaken Fortune's right hand in order to take a wanton giglot by the left hand."

In other words: Mosbie has not taken the right hand of Lady Fortune, who could have helped him; instead, he had taken the left hand of a lecherous whore — Alice's left hand.

Mosbie continued:

"I left the marriage of an honest maiden, whose dowry would have outweighed all thy wealth, whose beauty and demeanor far exceeded thee."

Mosbie was saying that he could have married a chaste virgin whose dowry, beauty, and behavior would have been better than those of Alice.

Mosbie continued:

"This certain good I lost in exchange for bad, and I wrapped and compromised my credit in thy company."

Mosbie had entwined his good name with Alice.

Mosbie continued:

"I was bewitched — that is no theme only of thine, for it is mine, also. And thou unhallowedly — wickedly — have enchanted me."

Both Alice and Mosbie were regretting their relationship, and both were claiming that the other had enchanted him or her.

Mosbie continued:

"But I will break thy spells and exorcisms — conjurations — and put another sight upon these eyes that showed my heart a raven for a dove."

He had thought that he was getting a turtle-dove in Alice, but really he was getting a black and ugly raven.

Mosbie continued:

"Thou are not fair and beautiful; I did not really see thee until now. Thou are not kind; until now I did not know thee. And now that the rain has beaten and washed off thy gilt, thy worthless copper shows thee to be counterfeit and phony."

The metaphorical gilt was a thin covering of precious gold that covered and hid the non-precious copper.

Alice was like a counterfeit coin.

Mosbie continued:

"It doesn't grieve me to see how foul thou are, but it maddens me that I ever thought thee fair.

"Go, get thee gone, thou who ought to be a copesmate for thy hinds — a companion to thy servants. I am too good to be thy favorite."

Alice said:

"Aye, now I see, and too soon find true that which often has been told me by my friends: Mosbie does not love me except for my wealth, an assertion that being too incredible I never believed."

Mosbie started to leave.

Alice now changed direction. Instead of rejecting Mosbie, she would accept him and continue the relationship.

She said:

"Nay, hear me speak, Mosbie, a word or two. I'll bite my tongue if it speaks bitterly.

"Look me in the face, Mosbie, or I'll kill myself: Nothing shall hide me from thy stormy, angry look. If thou cry war, there is no peace for me; I will do penance for offending thee, and burn this prayer-book, wherein I here use the holy word that had converted me."

As penance for making Mosbie, she would burn her prayer book, which may be the *Book of Common Prayer*. It was in that book that she had read the words that converted her — that made her want to reject her immoral relationship and instead go back to being a chaste and loyal wife to Arden.

Alice continued:

"See, Mosbie, I will tear away the leaves, and all the leaves, and in this golden cover shall thy sweet phrases and thy letters dwell. And thereon I will chiefly meditate, and I will hold no other sect but such devotion."

Alice was willing to rip out the pages of the *Book of Common Prayer* and to replace them with Mosbie's letters and words of love. Mosbie's love would be her religion from now on.

Alice continued:

"Will thou not look? Is all thy love overwhelmed?

"Will thou not hear? What malice stops thine ears?

"Why don't thou speak? What silence ties thy tongue?

"Thou have been sighted as the keen-eyed eagle is and have heard as quickly and sharply as the fearful hare and have spoken as smoothly and suavely as an orator, when I have asked thee to see or hear or speak.

"And are thou sensible — conscious — in none of these? Do thou possess none of these senses?

"Weigh all good turns I have done for thee against this little fault, and you will see that I don't deserve Mosbie's muddy, sullen looks.

"A spring or pool once troubled is not muddy always. Be clear again; I'll never more trouble thee."

Mosbie said sarcastically:

"O no, I am a base artificer: a lowly craftsman.

"My wings are feathered appropriately for a lowly flight."

Mosbie was saying that he was not born high enough to associate with someone like Alice. He was still hurting from words she had spoken to him.

He continued:

"Mosbie? Bah! No, not for a thousand pounds. Make love to you?

"Why, it is unpardonable. We beggars must not breathe where gentle people of high birth are."

Alice said:

"Sweet Mosbie is as gentle — as honorable — as a king, and I am too blind to judge him otherwise.

"Flowers do sometimes spring in fallow lands, weeds spring in gardens, roses grow on thorns."

In other words: One's birth does not determine one's character. A lowly born person can be a rose; a highly born person can be a weed.

Alice continued:

"So, whatsoever my Mosbie's father was, Mosbie himself is valued as gentle by his worth."

Mosbie said:

"Ah, how you women can insinuate and ingratiate yourself and themselves and clear a trespass and excuse a transgression with your sweet-set tongue!

"I will forget this quarrel, gentle Alice, provided I'll be tested so no more."

Alice said, "Then with thy lips seal up this new-made match."

She wanted them to kiss.

Bradshaw entered the scene.

"Wait, Alice, here comes somebody," Mosbie said.

"How are thou now, Bradshaw?" Alice asked. "What's the news with you?"

"I have little news, but here's a letter that Master Greene importuned and asked me to give you," Bradshaw said while giving Alice the letter.

"Go in, Bradshaw; call for a cup of beer," Alice said. "It is almost supper-time; thou shall stay with us."

Bradshaw exited.

Alice read the letter out loud:

"*We have missed of our purpose at London but shall perform it by the way. We thank our neighbor Bradshaw for delivering the letter.*

"*Yours, Richard Greene.*"

In other words: They had not murdered Arden, but they would try again.

Earlier, *before* hiring the murderers Black Will and Shakebag, Dick Greene had given Bradshaw a letter to deliver.

Alice asked Mosbie:

"What does my love think about the tenor and content of this letter?"

"I would think well of it, if Arden's period of life were completed and expired," Mosbie said.

Alice said:

"Ah, I wish it were! Then comes my happy hour. Until then my bliss is mixed with bitter gall.

"Come, let us go in to avoid suspicion."

Mosbie said, "Aye, to the gates of death to follow thee."

— 3.6 —

Scene 9

Dick Greene, Black Will, and Shakebag stood together at Rainham Down in Kent. They were on the road to Faversham, and they wanted to murder Arden in a few minutes.

"Come, Will, see that thy tools — thy pistols — are ready!" Shakebag said. "Is thy gunpowder dank and wet, or will thy flint strike fire?"

Insulted by the insinuation that he did not take good care of the tools of his trade, Black Will said:

"Then ask me if my nose is on my face, or whether my tongue is frozen in my mouth.

"By God's wounds, here's a fuss! You would do best to swear me on the interrogatories — questions asked an accused person — to tell the truth as I answer these questions:

"How many pistols have I taken in hand?

"Do I love the smell of gunpowder?

"Can I tolerate the noise the dag — the pistol — will make?

"Will I close my eyes at the flashing of the gunfire as the pistol goes off?

"I ask thee, Shakebag, to let this answer thee: I have taken more purses in this down — in this hilly area — than thou have ever handled pistols in thy life."

Purses are bags for containing money.

Shakebag said:

"Aye, perhaps thou have picked more pockets in a throng of people than I have. But if I would brag about what booty I have taken, I think the surplus that's more than thine would amount to a greater sum of money than either thou or all thy kin are worth.

"By God's wounds, as I hate a toad, I hate them who carry a muscado — a musket — in their tongue, and scarcely a hurting weapon in their hand."

He hated people who were all talk and no experience.

Black Will said:

"O Greene, this is intolerable! It is not in accordance with my honor to bear this.

"Why, Shakebag, I did serve the king at Boulogne, and thou can brag of nothing that thou have done."

Shakebag said, "Why, so can Jack of Faversham, who fainted because of a fillip — a blow — on the nose, and then he who gave it to him yelled in his ear, and he supposed that a cannon-bullet had hit him."

Jack was a soldier who got hit in the nose and knocked unconscious by another soldier, who revived him by shouting in his ear. Once revived, Jack thought that he had been hit by a cannonball.

Dick Greene said:

"Please, sirs, listen to Aesop's talk: While two stout, brave dogs were striving for a bone, a cur came and stole it from them both."

Aesop wrote fables about animals. Each fable had a moral.

Black Will and Shakebag fought.

Dick Greene then said:

"So, while you stand striving on these terms of manhood, Arden escapes us, and he gets the best of us all."

"Why, Black Will began it," Shakebag said.

Black Will said:

"And thou shall find I'll end it; I do but let this slip by and pass until a better time.

"But if I do forget —"

He knelt down and held up his hands to Heaven as he prepared to make a mighty oath.

Dick Greene interrupted:

"Well, take your fittest standings, and once more lime well your twigs to catch this wearisome bird."

The "fittest standings" were the best places to stand to ambush Arden.

Birds were caught with sticky birdlime. Dick Greene was telling Black Will and Shakebag to get ready for the ambush.

Greene continued:

"I'll leave you, and at your dag's — your pistol's — discharge, I'll come towards you, like the longing water-dog that lies down until the fowling-piece goes off, and then seizes on the prey eagerly."

A water-dog retrieves game from ponds, rivers, and lakes.

A flowing-piece is a light gun for shooting birds.

Greene continued:

"Ah, I wish that I might see the dying Arden stretching forth his limbs in his dying throes, as I have seen dying birds beat their wings before now!"

"Why, that thou shall see, if he comes this way," Shakebag said.

"Yes, that he does, Shakebag, I assure thee," Dick Greene said. "But don't brawl when I am gone for any reason. But, sirs, be sure to speed him when he comes, and in that hope, I'll leave you for an hour."

He wanted Black Will and Shakebag to speed Arden on his way to death.

Dick Greene exited.

Arden, Franklin, and Michael entered the scene at a distance. They did not see Black Will and Shakebag, who were hiding.

"It would be best that I went back to Rochester," Michael said. "The horse limps downright — definitely; it would not be good that it travelled and travailed in such pain to Faversham. Removing a shoe may perhaps help it."

"Well, get back to Rochester," Arden said, "but, sirrah, see that you catch up with us before we come to Rainham Down, for it will be very late before we get home."

Rainham is a town between Rochester and Faversham. A "down" is rolling countryside.

Michael said to himself, "Aye, God knows, and so do Will and Shakebag, that thou shall never go further than that down. And therefore I have pricked the horse's hoof on purpose to make it lame, because I don't want to view the massacre."

Michael was afraid, too, that he might be one of the people who would be massacred.

Michael exited.

"Come, Master Franklin, carry on with your tale," Arden requested.

"I assure you, sir, that you ask me to do much," Franklin said. "A heavy, oppressive blood is gathered at my heart, and suddenly my breath is so short that it hinders the passage of my speech. So fierce a qualm of sickness never before now assailed me."

"Come, Master Franklin, let us go on more slowly: The annoyance of the dust or else some food you ate at dinner cannot put up with or make use of you

— that is, it cannot be digested by you. I have been often ill like that, and soon amended and felt better."

"Do you remember where my tale did leave off?" Franklin asked.

"Aye, where the gentleman did check and rebuke his wife," Arden said.

Franklin said, "She was reprehended and criticized for the deed, a witness was produced who had caught her in the act, her glove was brought in that she had left behind there, and also many other assuredly strong pieces of evidence were brought in, and after all this, her husband asked her whether she was guilty."

"What was her answer then?" Arden said. "I wonder how she looked, having forsworn it with such vehement oaths, and at the instant so proved the deed against her."

The woman had vehemently sworn that she had not done what she was accused of doing, but then evidence proved that she really had done that deed.

Franklin said:

"First, she cast her eyes down to the earth, watching the drops that fell in great numbers from thence. Then softly she drew forth her handkerchief, and she modestly wiped her tear-stained face.

"Then she ahemmed, to clear her voice it should seem, and with a majesty prepared herself to counter and meet all their accusations —

"Pardon me, Master Arden, I can continue no more.

"This fighting at my heart makes my breath short."

"Come, we are almost now at Rainham Down," Arden said. "Your pretty tale beguiles and makes short the weary way; I wish that you were in the right state and condition to tell it out."

"Stand hidden, Will," Shakebag said. "I hear them coming."

Lord Cheiny suddenly appeared with his men.

He said:

"Is it as near night as it seems, or will this black-faced evening have a shower?"

In other words: Is it already twilight, or has the sky darkened because of an imminent rain shower?

Seeing Arden and Franklin, he said:

"What! Master Arden? You are well met — it is good to meet you. I have longed for a fortnight to speak with you: You are a stranger, man, in the Isle of Sheppy — you should visit more often."

"Stand to it, Shakebag, and be resolute," Black Will said.

"I am your honor's always!" Arden said. "I am bound to do you service."

"Have you come from London, and brought no serving-man with you?" Lord Cheiny asked.

"My serving-man's coming a little after me, but here's my honest friend Franklin who came along with me," Arden said.

"I take you to be Lord Protector's follower," Lord Cheiny said to Franklin, recognizing him.

"Aye, my good lord," Franklin said, "and I am highly bound to you."

"You and your friend come home and dine with me," Lord Cheiny said to Arden.

"I beseech your honor to pardon me," Arden said. "I have made a promise to a gentleman, my honest friend, to meet him at my house. The occasion is of great importance, or else I would wait on you."

Arden wanted to go home. His honest friend was Franklin.

"Will you come tomorrow and dine with me, and bring your honest friend along with you?" Lord Cheiny said. "I have diverse matters to talk with you about."

"Tomorrow we'll wait upon your honor," Arden said.

Lord Cheiny said to his men:

"One of you stop my horse at the top of the hill."

Possibly, Lord Cheiny and his men had gotten off their horses while climbing a hill to avoid overtaxing their horses as they travelled 42 miles (68 km) — part of the distance would be on a ferry — from London to Lord Cheiny's home on the Isle of Sheppy.

Seeing Black Will, he said:

"What! Black Will? For whose purse are you waiting? Thou will be hanged in Kent when all is done."

"Not hanged, God save your honor," Black Will said. "I am your beadsman, and I am bound to pray for you."

Lord Cheiny said:

"I think thou never said a prayer in all thy life."

He said to his men:

"One of you give him a crown."

He then said to Black Will:

"And, sirrah, leave this kind of life. If thou should be tainted for a penny-matter — accused of even the smallest crime — and if thou come in question, surely thou will truss."

"Truss" meant "hang."

He then said:

"Come, Master Arden, let us be going. Your way and mine lie four miles together."

Lord Cheiny, his men, Arden, and Franklin exited, leaving Black Will and Shakebag behind.

Black Will said:

"May the devil break all your necks at four miles' end!

"By God's wounds, I could kill myself for very anger! His lordship intervenes, just when my dag — my pistol — was levelled at Arden's heart.

"I wish that Lord Cheiny's crown were molten down his throat."

The crown is the gold coin that Lord Cheney gave to Black Will.

Shakebag said:

"Arden, thou have wondrously holy luck. Did ever man escape as thou have done?

"Well, I'll discharge my pistol at the sky because by this bullet Arden shall not die."

He fired his gun.

Hearing the gunshot, Dick Greene returned and asked, "What! Is he down? Has he been dispatched?"

"Aye, he is dispatched in good health towards Faversham, to shame us all," Shakebag said.

"The devil he is!" Dick Green said, "Why, sirs, how did he escape?"

"When we were ready to shoot, my Lord Cheiny came and prevented his death," Shakebag said.

"The Lord of Heaven has preserved him," Dick Greene said.

Black Will said:

"Preserved a fig!

"The Lord Cheiny has preserved him and invites him to a feast to his house at Shorlow. But along the way once more I'll meet with him, and, even if all the Cheinys in the world say no, I'll have a bullet in his breast tomorrow.

"Therefore come, Greene, and let us go to Faversham."

"Aye, and excuse ourselves and apologize to Mistress Arden," Dick Greene said. "O, how she'll chafe and rage when she hears about this!"

"Why, I'll assure you that she'll think we don't dare to commit the murder," Shakebag said.

"Why, then let us go, and tell her all the matter, and plot a new plan to cut him off and kill him tomorrow," Black Will said.

CHAPTER 4
— 4.1 —
Scene 10

In a room in Arden's house at Faversham, Arden, Alice, Franklin, and Michael stood together. The time was the next morning, and the sun was rising.

Arden said:

"See how the Hours, the guardian of Heaven's gate, have by their toil removed the darksome clouds, so that Sol — the sun — may well discern the trampled path wherein he is accustomed to guide his golden car."

The Hours are goddesses of the seasons and guardians of the gates of Mount Olympus, home of the Olympian gods and goddesses.

The Sun-god drove the Sun-chariot across the sky each day. Currently, the sun was rising.

Arden continued:

"The season fits; the time is right. Come, Franklin, let's go away."

"I thought you did intend some special hunt that made you thus cut short the time of rest," Alice said.

"It was no chase — no hunt — that made me rise so early, but, as I told thee last night, to go to the Isle of Sheppy, there to dine with my Lord Cheiny," Arden said, "for so his honor recently commanded me."

Lord Cheney was an important man, and invitations given by him were not lightly to be declined.

Alice said:

"Aye, such 'kind' husbands seldom lack excuses: Home is a wild-cat to a wandering wit."

In other words: A restless mind does not want to stay at home.

Alice was putting on an act of wishing that her husband would stay home.

She continued:

"The time has been — I wish to God it were not past — that neither a title of honor nor a lord's command — neither a high-ranking official nor the invitation of a lord — could once have drawn you from these arms of mine.

"But my deserts — my good qualities — or your desires decay and diminish, or both; yet if true love may seem forsaken, I deserve still to have thy company."

"Why, please, sir, let her go along with us to Lord Cheiny's house," Franklin said. "I am sure his honor will welcome her and welcome us the more for bringing her along."

Arden said:

"I am happy to do that."

He ordered Michael:

"Sirrah, saddle your mistress' nag."

In. this society, a nag was a small riding horse; it was not necessarily old or feeble.

Michael exited.

"No, begged favor — a favor one has to ask for — merits little thanks," Alice said. "If I should go, our house would run away, or else be stolen; therefore, I'll stay behind."

"Nay, see how mistaken you are!" Arden said. "Please, go."

"No, no, not now," Alice said.

"Then let me leave thee satisfied in knowing this," Arden said. "Neither time nor place nor persons alter me, but that I hold thee dearer than my life."

"That will be shown by your quick return," Alice said.

"And that shall be before night, if I live," Arden said. "Farewell, sweet Alice, we intend to dine with thee."

Arden and Franklin would eat the midday meal with Lord Cheney, and then return home and eat the evening meal with Alice.

Alice exited, and Michael returned.

"Come, Michael, are our horses ready?"

"Aye, your horses are ready, but I am not ready," Michael said, "for I have lost my purse, with thirty-six shillings in it, while bringing my master's nag up from the pasture."

"I ask you to let us go ahead of Michael, while he stays behind to seek his purse," Franklin said.

Arden said to Michael, "Go and do it, sirrah, and see that you follow us to the Isle of Sheppy to my Lord Cheiny's, where we intend to dine."

Arden and Franklin exited.

Alone, Michael said to himself:

"So, may fair weather follow you, for ahead of you lies Black Will and Shakebag in the fenced-in field of broom. They are hidden, too well hidden for you. They'll be your ferrymen to your long home."

Broom is a species of brush.

A "long home" is a grave.

The ferryman is Charon, who in Greek and Roman mythology ferries souls to the Land of the Dead.

Clarke the painter entered the scene.

Seeing him, Michael said to himself:

"But who is this? The painter, my rival, who would necessarily win Mistress Susan."

"How are thou now, Michael?" Clarke asked. "How are my mistress and everyone else at home?"

His mistress is his loved one: Susan.

Michael asked, "Who? Susan Mosbie? She is your mistress, too?"

"Aye, how are she and all the rest doing?" Clarke asked.

"All are well except Susan," Michael said. "She is sick."

"Sick?" Clarke asked. "Of what disease?"

"Of a great fear," Michael said.

"A fear of what?" Clarke asked.

"Fear" means "dread," but "fear" sounds like "fere," which means "spouse." Michael was saying that Susan was ill because of fear that Clarke would be her spouse.

"A great fever," Michael answered.

"A fever?" Clarke said. "God forbid!"

"Yes, indeed, and a fever caused by a lurdan, too, as big as yourself," Michael said.

A "lurdan" is a loafer. In this society, a "fever-lurdan" is the "disease" of laziness.

Clarke said, "O, Michael, the spleen prickles and goads you: Your spleen is making you angry. Bah, you keep your eye on Mistress Susan."

"Indeed, to keep her from the painter," Michael said.

"Why more from a painter than from a serving-creature — a servant — like yourself?" Clarke asked.

"Because you painters make but a painting table — a board to paint on — of a pretty wench, and spoil her beauty by blotting her with paint," Michael said.

"What do you mean by that?" Clarke asked.

Michael said, "Why, that you painters paint lambs in the lining of wenches' petticoats, and we serving-men put horns to them to make them become sheep."

In this society, "mutton" is slang for "whore."

The serving-men use their "horns" to seduce the ladies and if the ladies are married to put horns on the head of their husbands — that is, they make the husbands cuckolds.

A jest of this society was about a painter who had to go overseas. Before he left, he painted a lamb on his wife's belly. A man committed adultery with her and used a brush to add horns to the lamb. When the painter-husband returned home after a year abroad, his wife told him that the lamb had grown up.

Michael updated the jest and had the painter paint the lamb on the lining of his wife's petticoat. It is unlikely that a wife would go over a year without washing her belly. A slovenly wife might go over a year without washing her petticoat.

"Such another word will cost you a cuff or a knock," Clarke said.

"Cuff" and "knock" are blows.

He was threatening to hit Michael.

Michael said:

"What, with a dagger made of a pencil?"

A "pencil" is a small paintbrush with a pointed tip.

Michael continued:

"Indeed, it is too weak, and therefore thou are too weak to win Susan."

"It" is probably the "pencil" located below Clarke's bellybutton.

"I wish that Susan's love lay upon this stroke," Clarke said.

He hit Michael's head and made it bleed.

He had made a vigorous stroke, and he wanted to make a vigorous sexual stroke with Susan.

Mosbie, Dick Greene, and Alice entered the scene.

Alice said:

"I'll bet my life that this fight is for Susan's love.

"Michael, did you stay behind your master for this purpose? Have you no other time to brabble and brawl in but now when serious matters are in hand?"

She then said:

"Tell us, Clarke, have thou done the thing thou promised?"

"Aye, here it is," Clarke said. "The very touch is death."

"It" is the poisoned crucifix that they had talked about earlier.

Alice said:

"Then this, I hope, if all the rest do fail, will catch Master Arden, and make him wise in death who lived a fool."

She then said to Mosbie:

"Why should he thrust his sickle in our corn and interfere with us, or what has he to do with thee, my love, or govern me, who is able to rule myself?"

In this society, a man was supposed to govern his wife. A good wife was an obedient wife.

She said sarcastically:

"Indeed, for credit's and reputation's sake, I must leave thee!"

She then said seriously to Mosbie:

"Nay, Arden must cease to live so that we may love, may live, may love; for what is life but love?

"And love shall last as long as life remains, and life shall end before my love depart."

Mosbie said:

"Why, what is love without true constancy and faithfulness?

"It is like a pillar built of many stones, yet neither with good mortar well-compacted nor with cement to fasten it in the joints, but that it shakes with every blast of wind, and being touched, immediately falls to the earth, and buries all its haughty pride in dust.

"No, let our love be rocks of adamant, which neither time nor place nor tempest can sunder and part."

"Adamant" was a legendary and very hard mineral.

Dick Greene said:

"Mosbie, stop making your declarations of love now, and let us think about what we have to do.

"I have placed Black Will and Shakebag in the field of broom. They are hidden and watching for Arden's coming; let's go to them and see what they have done."

75

Scene 11

Arden and Franklin stood together on the Kentish coast opposite the Isle of Sheppy. There was heavy fog, and they needed a ferry to take them to the island Lord Cheiny lived on.

"Oh, ferryman, where are thou?" Arden called.

Hearing the cry, the ferryman entered the scene and said, "Here, here, go ahead of me to the boat, and I will follow you."

"We have great haste," Arden said. "Please, come away."

"Bah, what a mist and fog are here!" the ferryman said.

"This mist and fog, my friend, are mystical, similar to a good companion's smoky, alcohol-soaked brain that was half drowned with new ale overnight," Arden said.

The companion's brain was "smoky" — that is, foggy.

Mystical language can be difficult to understand; so can be the language of a drunk.

"It would be a pity unless his skull were opened to make more chimney room," the ferryman said.

If the good companion's skull were opened, it would allow the alcoholic fumes in his brain to dissipate.

"Friend, what's thy opinion of this mist?" Franklin asked.

The ferryman said, "I think it is like a curst, shrewish wife in a little house, who never leaves her husband alone until she has driven him out of doors with her crying, wet pair of eyes; then he looks as if his house were on fire, or some of his friends were dead."

"Do thou speak this of thine own experience?" Arden asked.

"Perhaps, aye; perhaps, no: for my wife is as other women are, that is to say, governed by the moon," the ferryman said.

To be governed by the moon means to be changeable and fickle. But for women, it can also mean to have a menstrual cycle.

"By the moon?" Franklin asked. "How, I ask thee?"

"Nay, thereby lies a bargain, and you shall not have it fresh and fasting," the ferryman said.

"Fresh and fasting" means "eager and hungry" and "before eating."

In other words: I won't tell you for nothing. The ferryman wanted something in return for telling them.

"Yes, I ask thee to tell us, good ferryman," Arden requested.

"Then for this once let it be midsummer moon, but yet my wife has another moon," the ferryman said.

A midsummer moon is the moon at midsummer: June 24. Or it is the full moon nearest to midsummer.

A midsummer moon was thought to cause more madness than other moons. The ferryman is "mad" because he will give his passengers something for nothing.

The wife's "moon" is her vagina.

"Another moon?" Franklin asked.

"Aye, and it has influences and eclipses," the ferryman said.

"Influences" are ethereal fluids flowing down from the heavens. They were supposed to influence human behavior.

It can mean a fluid flowing in — in this case, semen.

The medieval Latin word *influentia* means "inflow."

"Eclipses" occur when the moon blocks the sun, or the earth's shadow falls on the moon.

Possibly, the ferryman's wife's eclipses are when she has her period and/or will not have sex with the ferryman.

"Why, then, by this reasoning you sometimes play the man in the moon?" Arden asked.

"Aye, but you had best not to meddle with that moon, lest I scratch you by the face with my bramble-bush," the ferryman said.

The man in the moon had a thorn-bush. One tradition states that the man in the moon was cutting thorn-bushes on the Sabbath, and as punishment he was put on the moon.

"I am almost stifled and suffocated with this fog," Arden said. "Come, let's go away."

"And, sirrah, as we go, let us have some more of your bold yeomanry," Franklin said to the ferryman.

He wanted to hear more of the ferryman's bold speech that was appropriate for a yeoman: a member of the working class who was under the rank of a gentleman.

"Nay, by my truth, sir, my speech is just flat knavery — crude jesting," the ferryman said.

— 4.3 —

Scene 12

Black Will and Shakebag met each other on the foggy Kentish coast.

"Oh, Will, where are thou?" Shakebag asked.

"Here, Shakebag, almost in hell's mouth, where I cannot see my way because of smoke," Black Will said.

Some entrances to the Land of the Dead were the mouths of caves that emitted poisonous vapors.

The "smoke" was the heavy fog.

"I ask thee to speak continually so that we may meet by the sound, for I shall fall into some drainage ditch or other, unless my feet see better than my eyes," Shakebag said.

The "sound" is the water between the shore and the Isle of Sheppy.

"Did thou ever see better weather to run away with another man's wife, or play with a wench at pot-finger?" Black Will asked.

"Pot-finger" is when a child puts a finger in his or her mouth.

Of course, Black Will had in mind a feminine "pot" and a male finger or "finger."

A "pot" can be a deep hole or a container.

Shakebag said:

"No, I haven't. This would be a fine world for chandlers — candle-makers and -sellers — if this weather would last; for then a man should never dine nor drink without candlelight.

"But, sirrah Will, what horses are those that passed?"

"Why, did thou hear any?" Black Will asked.

"Aye, that I did," Shakebag said.

"I bet my life against thine that it was Arden and his companion, and then all our labor's lost," Black Will said.

"Nay, don't say that, for if it is they, they may haply — perhaps and happily for us — lose their way as we have done, and then we may chance to meet with them," Shakebag said.

"Come, let us go on like a couple of blind pilgrims," Black Will said.

"Pilgrims" are travelers for religious reasons.

Shakebag fell into a water-filled drainage ditch.

"Help, Will, help," Shakebag shouted. "I am almost drowned."

Hearing Shakebag, the ferryman entered the scene and asked, "Who's that who calls for help?"

"It was no one here," Black Will said. "It was thou thyself."

The ferryman said:

"I came to help him who called for help."

Shakebag climbed out of the ditch and the ferryman said to him:

"Why, how are thou now? Who is this who was in the ditch? You are well enough served for going without a guide in such weather as this."

In other words: You have gotten what you deserved.

Black Will asked, "Sirrah, what groups of people have passed on your ferry this morning?"

"None but a couple of gentlemen, who went to dine at my Lord Cheiny's," the ferryman said.

"Shakebag, didn't I tell thee as much?" Black Will asked.

"Why, sir, will you have any letters carried to them?" the ferryman asked.

The ferry carried letters as well as passengers.

"No, sir; get you gone," Black Will said.

"Did you ever see such a mist as this?" the ferryman asked.

"No, nor such a fool as will rather be hocked — have his hamstrings cut — than get on his way," Black Will said.

"Why, sir, this is no Hock-Monday; you are deceived," the ferryman man said.

Hock-Monday is the second Monday after Easter. On Hock-Monday and Hock-Tuesday, people could be light-heartedly tied up and let go after a small sum of money for the parish church — or a kiss — was paid. As you would expect, on alternate days, men tied up women, and women tied up men. Travelers were also tied up.

The ferryman asked Shakebag about the insulting Black Will, "What's his name, I ask you, sir?"

"His name is Black Will," Shakebag said.

"I hope to see him one day hanged upon a hill," the ferryman said.

If he were hanged on a hill, lots of people would see him.

The ferryman exited.

"See how the sun has cleared the foggy mist, now that we have missed the mark of our intent," Shakebag said.

Dick Greene, Mosbie, and Alice entered the scene.

"Black Will and Shakebag, what are you doing here?" Mosbie asked. "What! Is the deed done? Is Arden dead?

Black Will said:

"What could a blinded man perform in arms? How could he use his weapons? Didn't you see how until now the sky was so dark that neither horse nor man could be discerned?

"Yet we did hear their horses as they passed."

"Have they escaped you, then, and passed the ferry?" Dick Greene asked.

"Aye, for a while; but here we two will stay, and at their coming back, we will meet with them once more," Shakebag said. "By God's wounds, I was never so toiled and exhausted in all my life in trying to accomplish so slight a task as this."

Mosbie asked Shakebag, "How came thou to be so berayed — so filthy and spattered with mud?"

"With making false footing in the dark," Black Will said. "He insisted on following them without a guide."

"Here's money to pay for a fire and good cheer," Alice said. "Get you to the Flower-de-Luce Inn in Faversham and rest yourselves until some other time."

She gave Black Will money.

"Leave it to me," Dick Greene said. "It most concerns my situation and reputation."

Greene was accepting responsibility for the failure of Black Will and Shakebag to kill Arden, but he still wanted to succeed in killing him.

"Aye, Mistress Arden, this money you gave us will serve the purpose, in case we fall into a second fog," Black Will said.

Dick Greene, Black Will, and Shakebag exited.

"These knaves will never do it," Mosbie said. "Let us give it over. Let's give up."

Alice said:

"First tell me how you like my new device: my new plot.

"Soon, when my husband is returning back, you and I both marching arm in arm, like loving friends — like lovers — we'll meet him on the way, and we'll boldly beard and brave him to his teeth."

They would insult him to his face.

To "beard" someone was to pull on their beard: a deadly insult.

Alice continued:

"When words grow hot and blows begin to rise, I'll call those cutters — those cut-throats — forth from your tenement — your dwelling — who, in a manner to take up and join the fray, shall wound my husband Hornsby to the death."

Black Will and Shakebag would join the fight and kill Arden.

"Hornsby" was an insulting nickname for Arden; "horns" referred to the invisible horns said to grow on the forehead of cuckolds.

"A fine plot!" Mosbie said. "Why, this deserves a kiss."

He and Alice kissed, and then they departed.

— 4.4 —

Scene 13

Dick Reede and a sailor who was his friend talked together in the open country. Dick Reade had lost his land to Arden.

"Indeed, Dick Reede, it is to little end," the sailor said. "His conscience is too liberal, and he is too niggardly to part from anything that may do thee good."

"Liberal" can mean "generous," but here it means "unrestrained," as in "unrestrained by morality."

According to the sailor, Arden was greedy and hoarded wealth rather than share with others.

Dick Reade said:

"He is coming from Shorlow — Lord Cheney's house — I understand. Here in the open I'll intercept him, for at his house he never will vouchsafe and agree to speak with me. If prayers and fair entreaties will not serve or will make no battery in his flinty breast — no impression on his hard heart "— I'll curse the carle — the churl, the base fellow — and see what that will do."

Franklin, Arden, and Michael entered the scene.

Dick Reade continued:

"See from where he comes to further my intention! I can now do what I was planning to do."

He then said:

"Master Arden, I am now going to the sea. My coming to you was about the plot of ground that you wrongfully detain from me. Although the rent of it is very small, yet it will help my wife and children, which here I leave in Faversham, God knows, needy and bare. For Christ's sake, let them have it!"

The small plot of ground was big enough to grow vegetables on and help feed Dick Reade's family while he was away and working as a sailor.

Arden said:

"Franklin, do thou hear this fellow speak? That which he craves, I dearly — expensively — bought from him, although the rent-income from it was always mine."

According to Arden, he had bought the land from Dick Reade. Now Dick Reade was regretting the sale.

The dissolution of the monasteries caused hardship for many people. Some people were forced to accept money for lands they used although they preferred to keep the use of the land.

Arden then said to Dick Reade:

"Sirrah, you who ask these questions, if with thy clamorous impeaching — loudly accusing — tongue thou rail on me, as I have heard thou do, I'll lay thee up so close a twelve-month's day, as thou shall neither see the sun nor see the moon."

Arden was threatening to have Dick Reade imprisoned for a year.

Arden continued:

"Look to it, for, as surely as I live, I'll banish pity and show no mercy if thou treat me like this."

Dick Reade said:

"What! Will thou do me wrong and threaten me, too? Nay, then, I'll tempt and provoke thee, Arden, to do thy worst."

"I beseech thee, God, to show some miracle on thee, Arden, or on thine family — by plaguing thee, Arden, for this."

He then cursed Arden:

"May that plot of ground which thou withhold from me — I speak it in an agony of spirit — be ruinous and fatal unto thee!

"Either thou be butchered there by thy dearest friends ...

"Or else thou be brought there and put on public display for men to wonder at ...

"Or thou or thine miscarry and come to harm in that place ...

"Or thou there run mad and end thy cursed days!"

Franklin said to Dick Reade, "Bah, bitter knave, bridle thine malicious tongue. For curses are like arrows shot upright, which falling down alight on the shooter's head."

A proverb stated, "Curses return upon the heads of those who curse."

Dick Reade said:

"Let them alight where they will!

"If I were upon the sea, as often I have been in many a bitter storm, and saw a dreadful southern squall of wind at hand, the pilot quaking at the frightful storm, and all the sailors praying on their knees, even in that fearful time I would fall down, and ask God, whatever happens to me, to wreak vengeance or some misfortune on Arden to show the world what wrong the carle — the churl — has done.

"This order I'll leave with my distressed wife: My children shall be taught such prayers as these.

"And thus I go, but I leave my curse with thee."

Dick Reede and the sailor exited.

"He is the railingest knave in Christendom, and often the villain is a lunatic," Arden said. "It does not greatly matter what he says. But I assure you I never did him wrong."

"I think so, too, Master Arden," Franklin said. "I believe you."

"Now that our horses have gone home ahead of us, my wife may perhaps come and meet me on the way," Arden said. "For God knows she has grown surpassingly kind to me recently, and she has greatly changed from the old moods of her accustomed forwardness and willfulness, and she seeks by fair means to make amends for her old faults."

Franklin said:

"Happy is the change that alters for the best!

"But see in any case you don't talk about the meal and entertainment we had at my Lord Cheiny's, although it was most bounteous and generous, for that will make her think herself more wronged, in that we did not bring her along. For I am sure she grieved that she was left behind."

"Come, Franklin, let us strain to mend — pick up — our pace, and take her unawares playing the cook and making a meal at home," Arden said, "for I believe she'll strive to mend — improve — our cheer."

"Why, there's no better creatures in the world than women are when they are in good moods," Franklin said.

Alice and Mosbie entered the scene. Their arms were intertwined, and they kissed.

Arden said:

"Who is that? Mosbie? What! So familiar with my wife?

"Injurious strumpet, and thou ribald, irreverent knave, untwine those arms."

A strumpet is a whore.

"Aye, with a sugared kiss, let them untwine," Alice said.

Arden said:

"Ah, Mosbie! Perjured beast!

"Bear this and bear all!"

Mosbie had told Arden earlier that he was not having an affair with his wife. His actions now showed that he was a perjurer.

The expression "bear this and bear all" means: If I tolerate this, then I will tolerate anything.

"And yet I am no horned beast," Mosbie said. "The horns are thine."

The horns are those of a cuckold.

"O monstrous!" Franklin said. "Nay, then it is time to draw."

Arden and Franklin drew their swords.

"Help, help!" Alice shouted. "They murder my husband!"

This was the cue for Will and Shakebag, who entered the scene.

"By God's wounds, who injures Master Mosbie?" Shakebag asked.

He regarded Mosbie as Alice's "husband."

The men fought. Shakebag and Mosbie were wounded.

Shakebag said, "Help, Will! I am hurt!"

"I may thank you, Mistress Arden," Mosbie said, "for this wound."

Mosbie, Black Will, and Shakebag exited.

Alice said:

"Ah, Arden, what folly blinded thee? Ah, jealous harebrained man, what have thou done!

"When we, Mosbie and me, to welcome thee with sport and entertainment, came lovingly to meet thee on thy way—"

Her words were ambiguous: 1) She and Mosbie wanted to provide loving entertainment for Arden, or 2) She and Mosbie wanted to lovingly enjoy sexual sport and entertainment for themselves, and they wanted Arden to see them.

Alice continued:

"— thou drew thy sword, enraged with jealousy, and hurt thy friend Mosbie whose thoughts were free from harm.

"Thou did all this because of a meaningless kiss and the joining of arms, both done only merrily and in jest to test thy patience. And thou made unhappy me, who devised the jest, which, though begun in sport, yet ends in blood!"

"By the Virgin Mary, may God defend me from such a jest!" Franklin said.

Alice said to Arden:

"Couldn't thou see us friendly smile on thee, when we joined arms, and when I kissed his cheek? Haven't thou recently found me extremely kind to thou?

"Didn't thou hear me cry that they murder thee? Didn't I help to set my husband free?

"No, ears and all were bewitched; ah, I am accursed to link in liking — to fall in love — with a frantic man!

"Henceforth I'll be thy slave, no more thy wife, for with that name of 'wife,' I never shall content thee.

"If I am merry, thou immediately think that I am light and wanton.

"If I am sad, thou say the sullens trouble me and make me sad.

"If I am well-attired, thou think I will be gadding about.

"If I dress plainly, I seem sluttish — untidy and slovenly — in thine eye.

"Thus I am always and shall be until I die. Poor wench abused by thy misgovernment, mismanagement, and misbehavior!"

"But is it the truth that neither thou nor he intended malice in your misconduct?" Arden asked.

"The heavens can witness our harmless thoughts!" Alice said.

"Then pardon me, sweet Alice, and forgive this fault!" Arden said. "Forget just this and never again see the like. Impose on me a penance, and I will perform it, for in thy discontent I find a death — a death more tormenting than death itself."

Alice said:

"Nay, if thou had loved me as thou pretend to do, thou would have paid attention to the speeches of thy friend Mosbie; going wounded from the place here, he said that his skin was pierced only through my action.

"If sad sorrow taint thee for this fault, thou would have followed him, and seen his wounds taken care of, and asked for forgiveness from him whom thou have wronged.

"Never shall my heart be eased until this is done."

Arden said:

"Be happy, sweet Alice; thou shall have thy will, whatever it is. Because I injured thee, and wronged my friend, shame scourges and punishes me for my offence.

"Come thou thyself, and go along with me, and be a mediator between us two."

"Why, Master Arden!" Franklin said. "Do you know what you are doing? Will you follow him who has dishonored you by cuckolding you?"

"Why, can thou prove I have been disloyal?" Alice asked.

"Why, Mosbie taunted your husband with the horn," Franklin said. "Mosbie said that your husband was a cuckold."

"Aye, after Arden had reviled him with the injurious name of 'perjured beast,'" Alice said. "Mosbie knew no wrong could spite a jealous man more than the hateful naming of the horn."

"Suppose it is true," Franklin said, "yet it is dangerous to follow him whom he has recently hurt."

Alice said, "A fault confessed is more than half amends, but men of such ill-spirit as yourself work crosses and debates — create trouble and quarreling — between man and wife."

"Please, gentle Franklin, hold thy peace and don't say anything," Arden said. "I know my wife counsels me for the best. I'll seek out Mosbie where his wound is being taken care of, and salve and heal this unlucky and unfortunate quarrel if I may."

Arden and Alice exited.

Alone, Franklin said to himself:

"He whom the devil drives must go of necessity.

"Poor gentleman, how quickly he is bewitched! And yet, because his wife is the bewitcher, his friends must not be lavish in their speech. I must keep silent."

CHAPTER 5
— 5.1 —
Scene 14

Black Will, Shakebag, and Dick Greene talked together on a street in Faversham. Shakebag's arm was bandaged.

"Sirrah Greene, when was I so long in killing a man?" Black Will asked.

"I think we shall never do it," Dick Greene said. "Let's give it up."

"Nay, by God's wounds!" Shakebag said. "We'll kill him, even if we are hanged at his door for our labor."

Black Will said:

"Thou know, Greene, that I have lived in London these twelve years, where I have made some walk upon wooden legs for taking the wall on me."

If two men passed each other, the higher-ranking man would be closer to the wall, and the lower-ranking man would be closer to the dirty street. Black Will insisted on taking the side closer to the wall, and he claimed to have cut off the legs of men who attempted to take the wall side when passing him.

Black Will continued:

"I have made many go with silver noses for saying, 'There goes Black Will!'"

He also claimed to have cut off many noses because their owners said something he disliked, such as pointing out to law officers where he was fleeing. These men then were forced to use silver prostheses.

Black Will continued:

"I have cracked as many blades as thou have done nuts."

To "crack a blade" means to "break a sword," presumably while fighting. Or it means "To strike with a sharp noise," according to the *Oxford English Dictionary*.

"O monstrous lie!" Dick Greene said.

Black Will said:

"Truly, in a manner I have."

He was admitting that he had exaggerated.

Black Will continued:

"The bawdy-houses have paid me tribute."

Whore-houses paid him protection money.

Black Will continued:

"There dares not a whore to set up business, unless she has agreed with me first for opening her shop-windows."

He enjoyed a whore's services before she set up shop.

Black Will continued:

"For a cross word from a tapster — a bartender — I have pierced one barrel after another with my dagger and held him by the ears until all his beer has run out.

"In Thames Street a brewer's cart hauling alcohol was likely to have run over me. I made no more ado than going to the clerk and cutting all the notches of his tallies and beating them about his head."

Debts were recorded by making notches on sticks. Black Will ruined the notches and then used the sticks to beat the clerk who kept track of finances. With the notches ruined, the debt was uncollectable.

Black Will continued:

"I and my company have taken the constable from his watch and carried him about the fields on a coltstaff."

A coltstaff is a large staff, carried by two people, normally used for carrying large burdens other than constables.

Black Will continued:

"I have broken a sergeant's head with his own mace and bailed out and freed whom I wished with my sword and buckler."

Sergeants are police officers with the power to arrest malefactors.

A mace is a club or staff of office.

A buckler is a small shield.

Black Will continued:

"All the tenpenny-alehouse tapsters would stand every morning with a quart-pot in their hand, saying, 'Will it please your worship to drink?'"

Black Will drank for free because bartenders feared him.

Black Will continued:

"A tapster who had not done so would have been sure to have had his sign pulled down and his lattice window borne away the next night."

Inns usually had a lattice window painted red or green to identify the building as an inn.

Black Will continued:

"To conclude, what haven't I done? Yet I cannot do this; doubtless, he is preserved and kept alive by miracle."

Alice and Michael entered the scene.

"Hence, Will!" Dick Greene said. "Here comes Mistress Arden."

Dick Greene, Black Will, and Shakebag did not want to go up to her yet, so they withdrew a little distance away.

"Ah, gentle Michael, are thou sure they're friends?" Alice asked.

She was talking about Arden and Mosbie.

Michael said:

"Why, I saw them when they both shook hands. When Mosbie bled, Arden even wept for sorrow, and railed against Franklin as the cause of it all.

"No sooner came the surgeon in at doors, but my master — Arden — took to his purse and gave him money."

The surgeon is a doctor, not necessarily educated at a university.

Michael concluded:

"And, to conclude, Arden sent me to bring you word that Mosbie, Franklin, Bradshaw, Adam Fowle of the Flower-de-Luce Inn, with other of Arden's neighbors and his friends, will come and dine with you at our house this night."

Alice said:

"Ah, gentle Michael, run back again, and, when my husband walks into the fair — Faversham's St. Valentine's Fair — tell Mosbie to sneak away from him and come to me.

"And this night shall thou and Susan be made sure: You two shall be officially engaged."

"I'll go and tell him," Michael said.

"And as thou go, tell John the cook about our guests, and tell him to lay it on and spare no cost to make an excellent meal," Alice said.

Michael exited.

Black Will said to himself:

"Nay, if there will be such food and drink, we will invite ourselves."

Her then said:

"Mistress Arden, Dick Greene and I intend to sup with you."

"And welcome you shall be," Alice said.

Normally, a lower-class person such as Black Will inviting himself to a middle-class dinner would be rebuffed.

Alice continued:

"Ah, gentlemen, how did you miss your purpose last night? How did you fail to murder Arden?"

"It was on account of Shakebag, that unlucky villain," Dick Greene said.

"Thou do me wrong," Shakebag said. "I did as much as anyone else."

Black Will said:

"Nay then, Mistress Arden, I'll tell you what happened.

"When he should have locked in battle and crossed swords with both his hilts, Shakebag in a bravery flourished his sword over his head."

Shakebag may have been fighting with sword and dagger; thus, he would have two hilts. But instead of attacking immediately, he had made a show of bravado by whirling his sword over his head. This allowed Franklin, the man opposed to him, to attack him.

Black Will continued:

"Then Franklin came at Shakebag vigorously and hurt the slave; with that Shakebag slunk away.

"Now what he should have done was to have come at his opponent hand and feet, one and two, and thrusting his sword full out directly at his enemy's costard — head. But he like a fool bore his sword-point half a yard out of danger where it could do no good.

"I lie here to save my life."

It sounded as if he had pretended to be dead to save his life, or as if he were lying now to preserve his reputation as a badass.

"Lie" is also a position.

Black Will demonstrated a defensive posture and position.

Black Will continued:

"If the devil come, and if he has no more strength than defense, he shall never beat me from this ward: this defensive position."

Hmm. But if the devil would come in with offensive rather than defensive strength, probably the devil would defeat Black Will.

Black Will continued:

"I'll withstand his attack and maintain the defense. A buckler in a skillful hand is as good as a castle; nay, it is better than a sconce, for I have tried it."

A "buckler" is a small shield; a "sconce" is 1) a small fort, 2) a head, or 3) a helmet.

Although Black Will talked about maintaining his defense, he was supposed to be on offense: three against two. Mosbie, Shakebag, and Black Will against Arden and Franklin.

He was stressing his defense as a way of deflecting attention from his lack of offense.

Black Will continued:

"Mosbie, seeing all of Shakebag's defeat, began to faint: to lose courage.

"With that, Arden came with his arming — attacking — sword, and thrust him through the shoulder in a trice."

Arden's sword was not just for show; it was a real weapon.

Alice said, "Aye, but I wonder why you both stood still."

Black Will and Shakebag had performed poorly.

"Indeed, I was so amazed and stunned, I could not strike," Black Will said.

"Ah, sirs, had he last night been slain, for every drop of his detested blood I would have crammed angels in thy fist, and kissed thee, too, and hugged thee in my arms," Alice said.

"Be patient, we cannot help it now," Black Will said. "Greene and we two will dog and follow him through the fair, and stab him in the crowd, and steal away."

His shoulder bandaged, Mosbie entered the scene and walked over to them.

Alice said:

"It is impossible; but here comes he who will, I hope, invent some surer means.

"Sweet Mosbie, hide thy arm. It kills my heart."

"Aye, Mistress Arden, this bandage is your favor," Mosbie said.

In medieval times, a favor was a small possession such as a glove or a handkerchief that a lady gave a knight to wear on his arm or helmet.

Alice said:

"Ah, don't say that, for when I saw thee hurt, I could have taken the weapon thou let fall, and run at Arden; for I have sworn that these my eyes, offended with his sight, shall never close until Arden's eyes are shut up.

"This past night I rose and walked about the bedchamber, And twice or thrice I thought to have murdered him."

"What! In the night?" Mosbie said. "Then we would have been undone and ruined."

"Why, how long shall he live?" Alice asked.

Mosbie said:

"Indeed, Alice, no longer than this night.

"Black Will and Shakebag, will you two perform the plot that I have laid?"

"Aye, or else think of me as a villain," Black Will said.

"And rather than you shall fail in the plot, I myself will help, too," Dick Greene said.

Mosbie said:

"You, Master Greene, shall single Franklin forth, separating him from the others, and hold him with a long tale of strange news, so that he may not come home until supper-time.

"I'll fetch Master Arden home, and we, as friends do, will play a game or two at tables — at backgammon — here."

"But what is the point of all this?" Alice asked. "How shall he be slain?"

"Why, Black Will and Shakebag locked within the counting-house — the room that is used as an office — shall rush forth when a certain watchword is given," Mosbie said.

"What shall the watchword be?" Black Will said.

Mosbie said, "'Now I take you': That shall be the word. But no matter what, don't come forth before you hear the watchword."

"Now I take you" means 1) "Now I take all your game pieces and win the game," and 2) "Now I take your life."

"I assure you that we won't," Black Will said. "But who shall lock me in?"

"That I will do," Alice said. "Thou shall keep the key thyself."

Mosbie said:

"Come, Master Greene, go along with me.

"See that all things are ready, Alice, for when we come."

Alice said:

"Don't worry about that; send Arden home."

Mosbie and Dick Greene exited.

Alice then said:

"And if he ever goes forth out of his house alive again, blame me.

"Come, Black Will, who in my eyes are fair and attractive. Next after Mosbie I honor thee. Instead of fair words and large promises, my hands shall play you golden harmony."

The golden harmony is the clinking of gold coins.

"How do you like this? Tell me, will you do it, sirs?"

Black Will said:

"Aye, and that splendidly, too.

"Listen to my plan:

"Place Mosbie, being a stranger, in a chair."

By "stranger," Black Will meant "guest."

Chairs were rare in this society, and they were used mainly by the head of household, who could offer it to a special guest. Most people sat on stools and benches.

Black Will continued:

"And let your husband sit upon a stool, so that I may come behind Arden cunningly and without him seeing me, and with a hand-towel pull him to the ground, and then stab him until his flesh is like a sieve.

"That done, I will carry him behind the Abbey, so that those who find him murdered may suppose some slave or other killed him for his gold."

"A fine plan!" Alice said. "You shall have twenty pounds, and when he is dead, you shall have forty more, and, lest you might be suspected staying here, Michael shall saddle for you two vigorous geldings — castrated horses — to ride to where you will, to Scotland, or to Wales, I'll see you shall not lack for money, wherever you are."

"Such words would make one kill a thousand men!" Black Will said. "Give me the key. Which door leads to the counting-house?"

As mistress of the house, Alice carried the keys around with her. She gave Black Will the key to the counting-house, the door to which she pointed out.

"Here I would stay and continue to encourage you, except that I know how resolute you are," Alice said.

"Bah, you, Alice, are too faint-hearted," Shakebag said. "We must do this murder."

"But Mosbie will be there, whose very looks will add unaccustomed courage to my thought and make me the first who shall dare to attack him," Alice said.

"Bah, get you gone," Black Will said. "It is we who must do the deed. When this door opens next, look for his death."

Black Will and Shakebag went into the counting-house.

Alone, Alice said to herself:

"Ah, I wish that Arden were here now so that the door might open and Black Will and Shakebag come out to murder him!

"I shall no more be enclosed in Arden's arms that like the snakes of black Tisiphone sting me with their embracings!"

Tisiphone was a Fury, a mythological avenging spirit with snakes entwined in her hair. The Furies avenged people who were killed by family members. For example, they pursued Orestes after he killed his mother: Clytemnestra.

The stinging of Tisiphone's snakes was intended to stir up remorse and guilt for misdeeds.

Alice continued saying to herself:

"Mosbie's arms shall encompass me, and, if I were made a star, I would have no other spheres but those."

Mosbie's arms around her made a sphere, or circle.

The medieval view of the universe was that the Earth is at the center of the universe, and around the Earth are a number of crystalline spheres in which are embedded the planets, the sun, and the stars.

Alice continued saying to herself:

"There is no nectar but in Mosbie's lips!"

Nectar is the drink of the gods.

Alice continued saying to herself:

"Had chaste Diana kissed him, she like me would grow love-sick, and from her watery bower fling down Endymion and snatch Mosbie up."

Diana was a virgin goddess of the hunt who bathed in lakes and streams, and she was associated with the moon. The moon-goddess fell in love with Endymion. Here, Alice says that the moon-goddess, if she kissed Mosbie, would reject Endymion and instead take Mosbie as a lover.

Alice continued saying to herself:

"Then don't blame me, who will slay a silly, foolish man not half as lovely as Endymion."

Michael entered the scene and said, "Mistress, my master is coming near."

"Who comes with him?" Alice asked.

"Nobody but Mosbie," Michael said.

"That's well, Michael," Alice said. "Fetch in the tables, and when thou have done, stand before the counting-house door."

"Why?" Michael asked.

"Black Will is locked within to do the deed," Alice said.

"What!" Michael said. "Shall Arden die tonight?"

"Aye, Michael," Alice said.

"But won't Susan know it?" Michael asked.

"Yes, for she'll be as secret as ourselves," Alice said. "She won't talk."

"That's splendid," Michael said. "I'll go fetch the tables."

"But, Michael, listen to me a word or two," Alice said. "When my husband has come in, lock the street-door. He shall be murdered before the guests come in."

As the others talked, Michael exited and returned a few times, carrying tables and wine.

Arden and Mosbie entered the scene.

Alice said:

"Husband, what do you mean by bringing Mosbie home? Although I wished you to be reconciled, it was more out of fear for you than love of him. Black Will and Dick Greene are his companions, and they are cutters and may cut you short: Therefore, I thought it good to make you friends."

"Cutters" meant "throat-cutters."

Alice continued:

"But why do you bring him here now?

"You have given me my supper with his sight."

This is ambiguous. It can mean: 1) When I see him, I lose my appetite, or 2) My eyes feast on him.

"Master Arden, I think that your wife would have me gone," Mosbie said.

Arden said:

"No, good Master Mosbie; women will be prating.

"Alice, bid him welcome; he and I are friends."

"You may force me to do it, if you will," Alice said, "but I would rather die than bid him welcome. His company has purchased — acquired — for me ill friends, and therefore I will never frequent his company anymore."

Mosbie said to himself, "Oh, how cunningly she can dissemble!"

"Now that he is here, you will not treat me so," Arden said.

He wanted his wife to be a good hostess.

Alice said:

"I ask you not to be angry or displeased. I'll bid him welcome, seeing you'll have it so.

"You are welcome, Master Mosbie. Will you sit down?"

Mosbie said, "I know I am welcome to your loving husband, but as for yourself, you don't speak from your heart."

This was often true.

"And if I do not, sir, think that I have cause," Alice said.

"Pardon me, Master Arden," Mosbie said. "I'll go away."

"No, good Master Mosbie," Arden said.

Alice said to Mosbie, "We shall have guests enough, even though you go away from here."

"Please, Master Arden, let me go," Mosbie said.

"Please, Mosbie, let her prate her fill," Arden said.

"The doors are open, sir," Alice said. "You may leave."

Michael said to himself, "Nay, that's a lie, for I have locked the doors."

Arden said to Michael:

"Sirrah, fetch me a cup of wine. I'll make them friends."

Michael brought a cup of wine.

Arden then said:

"And, gentle Mistress Alice, seeing you are so stubborn, you shall begin and make the first toast! Don't frown. I'll have it so."

Alice said, "Please meddle with that which you have to do: Do what you have to do."

"Why, Alice! How can I do too much for him whose life I have endangered without cause?" Arden asked.

Alice said:

"It is true; and, seeing that it was partly through my means, I am happy to drink to him for this once."

Alice drank from the cup.

She then gave the drinking cup to Mosbie and said:

"Here, Master Mosbie! And please, henceforth be as strange to me as I am to you."

She meant: Be as passionate toward me as I am passionate toward you.

Alice continued:

"Your company has purchased me ill friends, and I for your account, God knows, have undeservedly been ill-spoken of in every place. Therefore henceforth frequent my house no more."

Mosbie said:

"I'll see your husband in spite of you.

"Yet, Arden, I protest to thee by Heaven, thou never shall see me anymore after this night."

Yes, if Arden is dead, he'll never see Mosbie again.

Mosbie continued:

"I'll go to Rome and convert to Catholicism rather than be forsworn by breaking my oath."

"Bah, I'll have no such vows made in my house," Arden said.

Alice said:

"Yes, please, husband, let him swear.

"And, on that condition, Mosbie, pledge and drink to me here."

"Aye, as willingly as I mean to live," Mosbie said.

"Come, Alice, is our supper ready yet?" Arden asked.

"It will be by the time you have played a game of backgammon," Alice said.

"Come, Master Mosbie, what shall we play for?" Arden asked.

"Three games for a French crown, sir, if it pleases you," Mosbie said.

"I am happy to do that," Arden said.

Mosbie and Arden played backgammon.

Black Will and Shakebag quietly came out of the counting-room behind Arden.

Black Will whispered to Alice, "Can't Mosbie win the game yet? What a spite is that!"

Alice whispered back, "Not yet, Will. Take heed he doesn't see thee."

"I fear he will spy me as I am coming," Black Will whispered.

"To prevent that, creep between my legs," Michael whispered to Black Will.

The word "between" may mean "behind."

Michael stood between Black Will and Arden's back, shielding Black Will.

"One ace, or else I lose the game," Mosbie said.

An "ace" is a snake-eye: the side with one dot.

Mosbie threw the dice.

"Ah, Master Arden, now I can take you," he said.

"By the Virgin Mary, sir," Arden said, "there's two to prevent failing."

Black Will, who had crept behind Arden, threw a hand-towel over his head and pulled him down.

Black Will and Shakebag were two men who would prevent the attempt at murder from failing.

"Mosbie! Michael! Alice!" Arden said. "What will you do?"

"Nothing but take you up, sir, nothing else," Black Will said.

"Take you up" can mean 1) bring you up short, 2) arrest you, 3) take you to Heaven, or 4) take a piece from the backgammon board.

"There's for the pressing iron you told me about," Mosbie, who had worked as a mender of clothing, said as he stabbed Arden.

"And there's for the ten pounds in my sleeve," Shakebag said as he stabbed Arden.

Alice said to her husband:

"What! Do thou groan?"

She said to Mosbie:

"Nay, then give me the weapon!"

Alice said as she stabbed her husband:

"Take this for hindering Mosbie's love and mine."

She stabbed Arden, and he died.

"O, mistress!" Michael said.

"Ah, that villain will betray us all," Black Will said.

"Bah, don't fear him," Mosbie said. "He will be secret."

"Why, do thou think I will betray myself?" Michael asked.

He could be executed for his part in the murder.

Shakebag said, "In Southwark dwells a bonny northern lass, the widow Chambly. I'll go to her house now, and if she will not give me harbor, I'll make booty of the quean — the whore — even to her smock. I'll rob her of everything except her underwear."

"Shift for yourselves; we two will leave you now," Black Will said.

"First lay the body in the counting-house," Alice said.

Black Will and Shakebag lay the body in the counting-house.

"We have our gold," Black Will said. "Mistress Alice, adieu. Mosbie, farewell, and Michael, farewell, too."

Black Will and Shakebag exited.

Susan entered the scene and said, "Mistress, the guests are at the doors. Listen, they knock. Shall I let them in?"

Alice said:

"Mosbie, go and bear them company."

Mosbie exited.

Alice then said:

"And, Susan, fetch water and wash away this blood."

Susan washed the floor, but she said, "The blood cleaves to the ground and will not come out."

Alice said:

"But with my fingernails I'll scrape away the blood."

Alice knelt and scraped the floor, but she said:

"The more I strive, the more the blood appears!"

"What's the reason, mistress?" Susan asked, "Can you tell?"

"Because I don't blush at my husband's death," Alice said.

The bloody floor was "blushing" for her.

Mosbie entered the scene and asked, "How are things now? What's the matter? Is all well?"

"Aye, well, if Arden were alive again," Alice said. "In vain we strive, for here his blood remains."

Already, she was regretting the murder.

Mosbie asked:

"Why, can't you strew rushes on it?"

Green rushes were strewn on floors as a covering.

He then said:

"This wench— Susan — does nothing. Fall to the work."

"It was thou who made me murder him," Alice said.

"What about that?" Mosbie asked.

"Nay, nothing, Mosbie," Alice said, "as long as it does not become known."

"Keep thou it secret, and it is impossible for it to become known," Mosbie said.

"Ah, but I cannot!" Alice said. "Wasn't he slain by me? My husband's death torments me at the heart."

"It shall not long torment thee, gentle Alice," Mosbie said. "I am thy husband; think no more about Arden."

Adam Fowle and Bradshaw entered the scene.

"How are thou now, Mistress Arden?" Bradshaw asked. "What illness makes you weep?"

"Because her husband is abroad so late," Mosbie said. "A couple of ruffians threatened him last night, and she, poor soul, is afraid he may be hurt."

"Is it nothing else?" Adam Fowle said. "Bah, he'll be here soon."

Dick Greene entered the scene and asked, "Now, Mistress Arden, do you lack any guests?"

"Ah, Master Greene, have you seen my husband lately?" Alice asked.

"I saw him walking behind the Abbey just now," Dick Greene said.

Franklin entered the scene.

Alice said:

"I do not like this being out so late.

"Master Franklin, where did you leave my husband?"

"Believe me, I haven't seen him since morning," Franklin said. "Don't be afraid. He'll come soon. In the meantime, you may do well to have his guests sit down."

Alice said:

"Aye, so they shall.

"Master Bradshaw, sit there."

She then said to Mosbie:

"Please, be content. I'll have my will. I insist. Master Mosbie, sit in my husband's seat."

This was the seat of honor.

"Susan, shall thou and I wait on them?" Michael whispered. "Or, if thou say the word, let us sit down, too."

If someone such as Mosbie could sit in the seat of honor, then servants ought to be allowed to sit at the table instead of serving others.

Susan whispered, "Peace, be quiet. We have other matters now in hand. I am afraid, Michael, that all will be betrayed."

Michael whispered:

"Bah, as long as it is known that I shall marry thee in the morning, I don't care although I should be hanged before night."

Previously, Michael had said that he believed that he could be saved from hanging if a virgin — Susan — offered to marry him.

Michael continued to whisper to Susan:

"But to prevent the worst, I'll buy some ratsbane — some rat poison."

"Why, Michael, will thou poison thyself?" Susan whispered.

"No, but I will poison my mistress, for I fear she'll tell," Michael whispered.

"Bah, Michael," Susan whispered. "Don't fear her; she's wise enough."

Mosbie said:

"Sirrah Michael, give us a cup of beer."

Michael gave him the beer.

Mosbie then said:

"Mistress Arden, here's to your husband."

"My husband!" Alice said.

"What ails you, woman, to cry so suddenly?" Franklin asked.

"Ah, neighbors, a sudden qualm came over my heart," Alice said. "My husband being forth torments my mind. I know something's amiss. He is not well, or else I would have heard about him before now."

Mosbie said to himself, "She will undo and ruin us through her foolishness."

"Don't be afraid, Mistress Arden," Dick Greene said. "He's well enough."

Alice said.

"Don't tell me that. I know he's not well. He was not accustomed to stay out thus late.

"Good Master Franklin, go and seek him, and if you find him, send him home to me, and tell him what a fear he has put me in."

Franklin said:

"I don't like this; I pray to God that all is well.

"I'll seek him and find him if I can."

Franklin, Mosbie, and Dick Greene exited.

Alice whispered, "Michael, what shall I do to get rid of the rest?"

Michael whispered to her:

"Leave that to my responsibility; let me do it."

He then said out loud:

"It is very late, Master Bradshaw, and there are many treacherous people outside, and you have many narrow lanes to pass."

Bradshaw said, "Indeed, friend Michael, what thou say is true. Therefore I ask thee to light us forth and lend us a link — lend us a torch."

Alice said:

"Michael, bring them to the doors, but do not stay. You know I do not love to be alone."

Bradshaw, Adam Fowle, and Michael exited.

Alice then said:

"Go, Susan, and bid thy brother Mosbie to come here. But why should he come? Here is nothing but fear.

"Stay, Susan, stay, and help to advise me."

"Alas! I advise you!" Susan said. "Fear frightens away my wits."

They opened the counting-house door and looked at Arden's corpse.

"See, Susan, where thy former master lies, sweet Arden, smeared in blood and filthy gore," Alice said.

"My brother, you, and I shall rue and regret this deed," Susan said.

"Come, Susan, help to lift his body out of the counting-house, and let our salt-tears be his obsequies — his funeral rites," Alice said.

Alice and Susan dragged Arden's body out of the counting-house.

Mosbie and Dick Greene returned.

"How are things now, Alice?" Mosbie asked. "To where will you carry him?"

"Sweet Mosbie, have thou come?" Alice said. "Then weep who will. I have my wish in that I enjoy thy sight."

"Well, it behooves us to be circumspect and cautious," Dick Greene said.

"Aye, for Franklin thinks that we have murdered him," Mosbie said.

"Aye, but he cannot prove it for his life," Alice said. "We'll spend this night in dalliance and in sport: in flirting and fun."

Michael returned and said, "O mistress, the mayor and all the night-watchmen are coming towards our house with glaives and bills."

Glaives and bills are weapons. A glaive is 1) a sword, or 2) a staff with a blade at one end: It is a sword-blade on a long pole-arm. A bill is a staff with a hook and spikes at one end. It is similar to a halberd.

"Make the door fast and lock it," Alice said. "Don't let them come in."

Michael left and locked the street door, and then he returned.

"Tell me, sweet Alice. How shall I escape?" Mosbie said.

"Go out at the back-door, go over the pile of wood in the yard, and for one night stay at the Flower-de-Luce Inn," Alice said.

"That is the best way to betray myself," Mosbie said.

"Alas, Mistress Arden, the night-watch will find and arrest me here, and that will cause suspicion," Dick Greene said. "There would be no suspicion if I were elsewhere."

"Why, take that way that Master Mosbie does," Alice said, "but first convey the body to the fields."

Everyone except Alice carried out Arden's body while Alice waited uncomfortably. They also carried out the murder weapon and a bloodstained hand-towel.

Everyone except Michael and Susan returned.

Mosbie said, "Until tomorrow, sweet Alice. Now farewell, and see that you confess nothing, no matter what."

"Be resolute, Mistress Alice," Dick Greene said. "Don't betray us but cleave and stick to us as we will cleave and stick to you."

Mosbie and Dick Greene exited.

"Now, let the judge and juries do their worst," Alice said. "My house is clear, and now I don't fear them."

"Clear" can mean 1) unsullied, 2) free from guilt, and/or 3) without a corpse.

Michael and Susan returned. Michael's responsibilities had included the additional job of getting rid of the knife and the hand-towel.

"As we went, it snowed all the way, which makes me fear our footsteps will be spied and seen," Susan said.

"Peace, fool, be quiet," Alice said. "The snow will cover them again."

"But the snow had finished before we came back again," Susan said.

Knocking on the door sounded.

Alice said:

"Listen! Listen! They knock!

"Go, Michael, and let them in."

Michael let in the mayor and the night-watch.

Alice asked:

"How are things now, Master Mayor? Have you brought my husband home?"

"I saw him come into your house an hour ago," the mayor said.

"You are deceived," Alice said. "It was a Londoner."

"Mistress Arden, don't you know a man who is called Black Will?" the mayor asked.

"I know none such," Alice said. "What is the meaning of these questions?"

"I have the Council's warrant to apprehend and arrest him," the mayor said.

Alice said to herself:

"I am glad it is no worse."

She then said out loud:

"Why, Master Mayor, do you think I harbor any such man? Do I think that I am hiding and protecting him?"

"We are informed that here he is," the mayor said, "and therefore pardon us, for we must search."

Alice said:

"Aye, search, and don't spare searching anywhere. Go through every room. If my husband were at home, you would not attempt to do this."

Franklin returned.

Alice asked:

"Master Franklin, why have you come here so sad?"

"Arden, thy husband and my friend, has been slain," Franklin said.

"Ah, by whom?" Alice asked. "Master Franklin, can you tell?"

"I don't know; but behind the Abbey there he lies murdered in a most pitiful condition," Franklin said.

"But, Master Franklin, are you sure it is he?" the mayor asked.

"I am too sure," Franklin said. "I wish to God that I were deceived."

"Find out the murderers," Alice said. "Let them be known."

"Aye, so they shall," Franklin said. "You come along with us."

"Why?" Alice asked.

"Do you recognize this hand-towel and this knife?" Franklin asked.

"Ah, Michael, through this thy negligence, thou have betrayed and undone and ruined us all," Susan whispered.

It had been Michael's job to dispose of that evidence.

"I was so afraid that I didn't know what I did," Michael whispered. "I thought I had thrown them both into the well."

The hand-towel and knife were bloody.

Alice said:

"It is the pig's blood we had for supper."

Blood is an ingredient in some food.

Alice then said:

"But why do you stay here? Go and find the murderers."

"I am afraid that you'll prove to be one of them yourself," the mayor said.

"I one of them?" Alice said. "What is the meaning of such questions?"

Franklin said:

"I am afraid that he was murdered in this house and carried to the fields; for from that place backwards and forwards, you may see the prints of many feet within the snow.

"And look about this chamber where we are, and you shall find part of his guiltless, innocent blood, for in his slipshoe — his slipper — I found some rushes, which is evidence that he was murdered in this room."

The floor was covered with rushes.

The mayor said:

"Look in the place where he was accustomed to sit.

"See! See! His blood! It is too manifestly obvious."

"It is a cup of wine that Michael shed," Alice said.

That is, Michael had spilled a cup of wine.

In Matthew 26:28, Jesus said, "*For this is my blood of the new testament, which is shed for many for the remission of sins*" (King James Version).

"Aye, truly," Michael said.

"It is his blood, which, thou whore, thou have shed," Franklin said. "But if I live, thou and thy accomplices who have conspired and brought about his death shall rue and regret it."

"Ah, Master Franklin, God and Heaven can tell I loved him more than all the world," Alice said. "But bring me to him. Let me see his body."

"Bring that villain Michael and Susan — Mosbie's sister — too," Franklin said, "and one of you go to the Flower-de-Luce, and seek for Mosbie, and arrest him, too."

— 5.2 —

Scene 15

Alone, Shakebag stood on an obscure street in London.

He said to himself:

"I kept the widow Chambly as a mistress when her husband was still alive, and now that he's dead, she has grown so stout — so arrogant and proud — that she will not know her old companions.

"I came thither, thinking to have had safe harbor as I was accustomed to have, and she was ready to thrust me out of doors; but whether she would or not, I got up, and as she followed me, I spurned — kicked — her down the stairs, and broke her neck, and cut her tapster's throat, and now I am going to fling them in the Thames River."

Possibly, the tapster — a bartender — was a friend or new lover of hers.

Shakebag continued saying to himself:

"I have the gold. What do I care though the murders become known! I'll cross the water and take sanctuary."

Some religious places offered sanctuary: Criminals could not be arrested there.

— 5.3 —

Scene 16

The mayor, Mosbie, Alice, Franklin, Michael, and Susan stood in a room in Arden's house at Faversham. Arden's corpse was visible.

The mayor said, "See, Mistress Arden, where your husband lies. Confess this foul fault and be penitent."

Alice said:

"Arden, sweet husband, what shall I say?

"The more I speak his name, the more he bleeds. This blood condemns me, and in gushing forth it speaks as it falls, and it asks me why I did it."

In this society, people believed that a murder victim would bleed again in the presence of his or her murderer.

Genesis 4:9-10 (King James Version) states:

9) *And the LORD said unto Cain, Where is Abel thy brother? And he said, I know not: Am I my brother's keeper?*

10) *And he said, What hast thou done? the voice of thy brother's blood crieth unto me from the ground.*

Alice continued:

"Forgive me, Arden. I repent my sins now, and, if my death would save thine, thou should not die.

"Rise up, sweet Arden, and enjoy thy love, and don't frown on me when we meet in Heaven. In Heaven I do and will love thee, although on earth I did not."

According to Christian theology, repentant sinners go to Heaven.

"Tell us, Mosbie, what made thee murder him?" the mayor asked.

Franklin said to Mosbie:

"Don't think about how to answer the question; don't look down. His purse and girdle that were found at thy bed's head witness sufficiently that thou did the deed."

A girdle was a belt used to hold a purse, which held money.

Franklin continued:

"It is useless to swear thou didn't do it."

Mosbie said, "I hired Black Will and Shakebag, ruffians both, and they and I have done this murderous deed. But why do we stay and delay here? Come and take me away from here."

Actually, Dick Greene had hired the cutthroats. Mosbie wanted to get everything, including his own execution, over as quickly as possible.

Alice had also stabbed Arden, but Mosbie did not mention her.

"Those ruffians — Black Will and Shakebag — shall not escape," Franklin said. "I will go up to London and get the Privy Council's warrant to arrest them."

— 5.4 —

Scene 17

Black Will, alone on the Kentish coast, said to himself:

"Shakebag, I hear, has taken sanctuary, but I am so pursued with hues and cries for petty robberies that I have done, that I can come to no sanctuary."

A "hue and cry" is a loud cry to alert people to join in the chase after a criminal.

Black Will continued saying to himself:

"Therefore I must in some oyster-boat at last be satisfied to go onboard some hoy, and so go to Flushing."

Black Will was hoping to travel in an oyster-boat to get to someplace where he could get onboard a small passenger boat and go to Flushing in Holland.

Black Will continued saying to himself:

"There is no staying here.

"At Sittingburgh the watch was likely to take me, and if I hadn't with my buckler covered my head, and run full blank at all adventures —"

Black Will had covered his head with his shield and run recklessly as fast as he could.

Black Will continued saying to himself:

"— I am sure that I would have never gone further than that place. For the constable had twenty warrants to apprehend me.

"Besides that, I robbed him and his serving-man once at Gadshill.

"Farewell, England; I'll go to Flushing now."

Black Will exited.

— 5.5 —

Scene 18

The mayor, Mosbie, Alice, Michael, Susan, and Bradshaw walked into the justice-room at Faversham.

"Come, be quick and bring in the prisoners," the mayor said.

Bradshaw said:

"Mistress Arden, you are now going to God, and I am by the law condemned to die on account of a letter I brought from Master Greene.

"I ask you, Mistress Arden, to speak the truth: Was I ever privy to and in on the secret of your intention to murder your husband or not?"

Alice said:

"What should I say? You brought me such a letter, but I dare swear thou did not know the contents.

"Cease now to trouble me with worldly things, and let me meditate upon my savior Christ, whose blood must save me for the blood I shed."

If Bradshaw was innocent, Alice should speak up for him rather than worry about herself. A repentant sinner ought to be concerned about justice.

"How long shall I live in this hell of grief?" Mosbie said. "Convey me from the presence of that strumpet."

Mosbie and Alice no longer loved — or even liked — each other.

Alice said:

"Ah, except for thee I had never been a strumpet. What cannot oaths and protestations do when men have opportunity to woo?

"I was too young to sound out — to fathom — thy villainies, but now I find them and repent too late."

Mosbie and Alice were blaming each other for their troubles, but both had stabbed Arden.

Susan said to Mosbie, "Ah, gentle brother, why should I die? I didn't know about it until the deed was done."

"For thee I mourn more than for myself," Mosbie said. "But let that suffice. I cannot save thee now."

113

Michael said to Susan, "And if your brother and my mistress Alice had not promised me that I would marry you, I never would have given my consent to this foul deed."

The mayor said:

"Cease to accuse each other now; listen to the sentence I shall give.

"Bear Mosbie and his sister to London immediately, where they in Smithfield must be executed.

"Bear Mistress Arden to Canterbury, where her sentence is she must be burnt."

Alice was to be burned at the stake because she was guilty of petty treason: She had murdered her husband.

The mayor continued:

"Michael and Bradshaw in Faversham must suffer death."

"Let my death make amends for all my sins," Alice said.

"Curses upon women!" Mosbie said. "This shall be my swan song. But bear me away from here, for I have lived too long."

Mosbie's sister was a woman, so he was cursing her, too.

"Seeing no hope on earth, I see that in in Heaven is my hope," Susan said.

"Indeed, I don't care, seeing I die with Susan," Michael said.

"May my blood be on his head who gave the sentence," Bradshaw said.

"To speedy execution with them all!" the mayor said.

EPILOGUE

Franklin spoke the epilogue to you, the readers and audience:

"Thus have you seen the truth of Arden's death.

"As for the ruffians Shakebag and Black Will, the one — Shakebag — took sanctuary, and, after being sent for and leaving sanctuary, he was murdered in Southwark as he passed to Greenwich, where the Lord Protector stayed.

"Black Will was burned at the stake in Flushing on a scaffold.

"Dick Greene was hanged at the village of Osbridge in Kent.

"The painter fled and how he died we don't know.

"But this above the rest is especially to be noted:

"Arden lay murdered in that plot of ground which he by force and violence withheld unfairly from Dick Reede. And in the grass his body's print was seen two years and more after the deed was done.

"Gentlemen, we hope you'll pardon this naked, unadorned, straightforward tragedy, wherein no filed points — no elevated rhetorical devices — have been introduced to make it gracious and pleasing to the ear or eye, for simple truth is gracious and pleasing enough, and needs no other points of glozing — superficially attractive — stuff."

NOTE

— 1.1. —

mithridate

The name of this universal antidote comes from Mithridates, who inured himself to poison by taking a little of it and then a little more of it each following day.

The following lines of poetry come from the end of A.E. Housman's poem "Terence, This is Stupid Stuff" in his poetry collection *A Shropshire Lad*:

There was a king reigned in the East:
There, when kings will sit to feast,
They get their fill before they think
With poisoned meat and poisoned drink.
He gathered all that sprang to birth
From the many-venomed earth;
First a little, thence to more,
He sampled all her killing store;
And easy, smiling, seasoned sound,
Sate the king when healths went round.
They put arsenic in his meat
And stared aghast to watch him eat;
They poured strychnine in his cup
And shook to see him drink it up:
They shook, they stared as white's their shirt:
Them it was their poison hurt.
— I tell the tale that I heard told.
Mithridates, he died old.

APPENDIX A: ABOUT THE AUTHOR

It was a dark and stormy night. Suddenly a cry rang out, and on a hot summer night in 1954, Josephine, wife of Carl Bruce, gave birth to a boy — me. Unfortunately, this young married couple allowed Reuben Saturday, Josephine's brother, to name their first-born. Reuben, aka "The Joker," decided that Bruce was a nice name, so he decided to name me Bruce Bruce. I have gone by my middle name — David — ever since.

Being named Bruce David Bruce hasn't been all bad. Bank tellers remember me very quickly, so I don't often have to show an ID. It can be fun in charades, also. When I was a counselor as a teenager at Camp Echoing Hills in Warsaw, Ohio, a fellow counselor gave the signs for "sounds like" and "two words," then she pointed to a bruise on her leg twice. Bruise Bruise? Oh yeah, Bruce Bruce is the answer!

Uncle Reuben, by the way, gave me a haircut when I was in kindergarten. He cut my hair short and shaved a small bald spot on the back of my head. My mother wouldn't let me go to school until the bald spot grew out again.

Of all my brothers and sisters (six in all), I am the only transplant to Athens, Ohio. I was born in Newark, Ohio, and have lived all around Southeastern Ohio. However, I moved to Athens to go to Ohio University and have never left.

At Ohio U, I never could make up my mind whether to major in English or Philosophy, so I got a bachelor's degree with a double major in both areas, then I added a Master of Arts degree in English and a Master of Arts degree in Philosophy. Yes, I have my MAMA degree.

Currently, and for a long time to come (I eat fruits and veggies), I am spending my retirement writing books such as *Nadia Comaneci: Perfect 10*, *The Funniest People in Comedy*, *Homer's* Iliad: *A Retelling in Prose*, and *William Shakespeare's* Hamlet: *A Retelling in Prose*.

If all goes well, I will publish one or two books a year for the rest of my life. (On the other hand, a good way to make God laugh is to tell Her your plans.)

By the way, my sister Brenda Kennedy writes romances such as *A New Beginning* and *Shattered Dreams*.

APPENDIX B: SOME BOOKS BY DAVID BRUCE

Retellings of a Classic Work of Literature

Arden of Faversham*: A Retelling*

Ben Jonson's The Alchemist: *A Retelling*

Ben Jonson's The Arraignment, or Poetaster: *A Retelling*

Ben Jonson's Bartholomew Fair: *A Retelling*

Ben Jonson's The Case is Altered: *A Retelling*

Ben Jonson's Catiline's Conspiracy: *A Retelling*

Ben Jonson's The Devil is an Ass: *A Retelling*

Ben Jonson's Epicene: *A Retelling*

Ben Jonson's Every Man in His Humor: *A Retelling*

Ben Jonson's Every Man Out of His Humor: *A Retelling*

Ben Jonson's The Fountain of Self-Love, or Cynthia's Revels: *A Retelling*

Ben Jonson's The Magnetic Lady, or Humors Reconciled: *A Retelling*

Ben Jonson's The New Inn, or The Light Heart: *A Retelling*

Ben Jonson's Sejanus' Fall: *A Retelling*

Ben Jonson's The Staple of News: *A Retelling*

Ben Jonson's A Tale of a Tub: *A Retelling*

Ben Jonson's Volpone, or the Fox: *A Retelling*

Christopher Marlowe's Complete Plays: Retellings

Christopher Marlowe's Dido, Queen of Carthage: *A Retelling*

Christopher Marlowe's Doctor Faustus: *Retellings of the 1604 A-Text and of the 1616 B-Text*

Christopher Marlowe's Edward II: *A Retelling*

Christopher Marlowe's The Massacre at Paris: *A Retelling*

Christopher Marlowe's The Rich Jew of Malta: *A Retelling*

Christopher Marlowe's Tamburlaine, Parts 1 and 2: *Retellings*

Dante's Divine Comedy: *A Retelling in Prose*

Dante's Inferno: *A Retelling in Prose*

Dante's Purgatory: *A Retelling in Prose*

Dante's Paradise: *A Retelling in Prose*

The Famous Victories of Henry V: *A Retelling*

From the Iliad *to the* Odyssey: *A Retelling in Prose of Quintus of Smyrna's* Posthomerica

George Chapman, Ben Jonson, and John Marston's Eastward Ho! *A Retelling*

George Peele's The Arraignment of Paris: *A Retelling*

George Peele's The Battle of Alcazar: *A Retelling*

George Peele's David and Bathsheba, and the Tragedy of Absalom: *A Retelling*

George Peele's Edward I: *A Retelling*

George Peele's The Old Wives' Tale: *A Retelling*

George-a-Greene: *A Retelling*

The History of King Leir: *A Retelling*

Homer's Iliad: *A Retelling in Prose*

Homer's Odyssey: *A Retelling in Prose*

J.W. Gent.'s The Valiant Scot: *A Retelling*

Jason and the Argonauts: A Retelling in Prose of Apollonius of Rhodes' Argonautica

John Ford: Eight Plays Translated into Modern English

John Ford's The Broken Heart: *A Retelling*

John Ford's The Fancies, Chaste and Noble: *A Retelling*

John Ford's The Lady's Trial: *A Retelling*

John Ford's The Lover's Melancholy: *A Retelling*

John Ford's Love's Sacrifice: *A Retelling*

John Ford's Perkin Warbeck: *A Retelling*

John Ford's The Queen: *A Retelling*

John Ford's 'Tis Pity She's a Whore: *A Retelling*

John Lyly's Campaspe: *A Retelling*

John Lyly's Endymion, The Man in the Moon: *A Retelling*

John Lyly's Galatea: *A Retelling*

John Lyly's Love's Metamorphosis: *A Retelling*

John Lyly's Midas: *A Retelling*

John Lyly's Mother Bombie: *A Retelling*

John Lyly's Sappho and Phao: *A Retelling*

John Lyly's The Woman in the Moon: *A Retelling*

John Webster's The White Devil: *A Retelling*

King Edward III: *A Retelling*

Mankind: *A Medieval Morality Play* (A Retelling)

Margaret Cavendish's The Unnatural Tragedy: *A Retelling*

The Merry Devil of Edmonton: *A Retelling*

The Summoning of Everyman: *A Medieval Morality Play* (A Retelling)

Robert Greene's Friar Bacon and Friar Bungay: *A Retelling*

The Taming of a Shrew: *A Retelling*

Tarlton's Jests: A Retelling

Thomas Middleton's A Chaste Maid in Cheapside: *A Retelling*

Thomas Middleton's Women Beware Women: *A Retelling*

Thomas Middleton and Thomas Dekker's The Roaring Girl: *A Retelling*

Thomas Middleton and William Rowley's The Changeling: *A Retelling*

The Trojan War and Its Aftermath: Four Ancient Epic Poems

Virgil's Aeneid: *A Retelling in Prose*

William Shakespeare's 5 Late Romances: Retellings in Prose

William Shakespeare's 10 Histories: Retellings in Prose

William Shakespeare's 11 Tragedies: Retellings in Prose

William Shakespeare's 12 Comedies: Retellings in Prose

William Shakespeare's 38 Plays: Retellings in Prose

William Shakespeare's 1 Henry IV, aka Henry IV, Part 1: *A Retelling in Prose*

William Shakespeare's 2 Henry IV, aka Henry IV, Part 2: *A Retelling in Prose*

William Shakespeare's 1 Henry VI, aka Henry VI, Part 1: *A Retelling in Prose*

William Shakespeare's 2 Henry VI, aka Henry VI, Part 2: *A Retelling in Prose*

William Shakespeare's 3 Henry VI, aka Henry VI, Part 3: *A Retelling in Prose*

William Shakespeare's All's Well that Ends Well: *A Retelling in Prose*

William Shakespeare's Antony and Cleopatra: *A Retelling in Prose*

William Shakespeare's As You Like It: *A Retelling in Prose*

William Shakespeare's The Comedy of Errors: *A Retelling in Prose*

William Shakespeare's Coriolanus: *A Retelling in Prose*

William Shakespeare's Cymbeline: *A Retelling in Prose*

William Shakespeare's Hamlet: *A Retelling in Prose*

William Shakespeare's Henry V: *A Retelling in Prose*

William Shakespeare's Henry VIII: *A Retelling in Prose*

William Shakespeare's Julius Caesar: *A Retelling in Prose*

William Shakespeare's King John: *A Retelling in Prose*

William Shakespeare's King Lear: *A Retelling in Prose*

William Shakespeare's Love's Labor's Lost: *A Retelling in Prose*

William Shakespeare's Macbeth: *A Retelling in Prose*

William Shakespeare's Measure for Measure: *A Retelling in Prose*

William Shakespeare's The Merchant of Venice: *A Retelling in Prose*

William Shakespeare's The Merry Wives of Windsor: *A Retelling in Prose*

William Shakespeare's A Midsummer Night's Dream: *A Retelling in Prose*

William Shakespeare's Much Ado About Nothing: *A Retelling in Prose*

William Shakespeare's Othello: *A Retelling in Prose*

William Shakespeare's Pericles, Prince of Tyre: *A Retelling in Prose*

William Shakespeare's Richard II: *A Retelling in Prose*

William Shakespeare's Richard III: *A Retelling in Prose*

William Shakespeare's Romeo and Juliet: *A Retelling in Prose*

William Shakespeare's The Taming of the Shrew: *A Retelling in Prose*

William Shakespeare's The Tempest: *A Retelling in Prose*

William Shakespeare's Timon of Athens: *A Retelling in Prose*

William Shakespeare's Titus Andronicus: *A Retelling in Prose*

William Shakespeare's Troilus and Cressida: *A Retelling in Prose*

William Shakespeare's Twelfth Night: *A Retelling in Prose*

William Shakespeare's The Two Gentlemen of Verona: *A Retelling in Prose*

William Shakespeare's The Two Noble Kinsmen: *A Retelling in Prose*

William Shakespeare's The Winter's Tale: *A Retelling in Prose*